ONE VISIT

WRITTEN BY GEORGE VECK

ONE VISIT

Thanks to Jordan Tate and Bella Duve for beta reading.

Chapter 1 - Old School Kens

Frankie Gibbs' sunken eyes burst open. His underweight, sweaty midriff springs upwards and leans against the bed frame, panting and gasping for air. He's safe this time, although it takes him the thick side of sixty seconds to realize. He stretches over to his stale bedside half pint of water to sooth his parched throat. A desperate orange piss level of parched, amplified by shutting his stuffy room's windows to keep both spiders and next door's rotten month-old garden bin bag stench out. Not helped by his first sight of the day – a plethora of grubby beer cans and pot noodle packets varying in age – dread seeps in. To add insult to injury, a familiar warm sensation around his crotch area becomes increasingly apparent, a stinging itch on the thigh. An absolute disaster. The level of sting means only one thing, it happened early in the night, leaving more time for the piss to penetrate the plastic protection sheet and seep into the springy mattress. A peek under the covers at his drenched Primark pyjama bottoms confirms all suspicions, it's happened again. Undoubtedly, the chugging of eight pint cans of Galleryx lager during a Film4 Steven Seagal marathon headlined by On Deadly Ground played its part. Frankie gazes over to the corner of the room and grimaces, his clean sheet pile's as bare as his stomach. Barring a

5

miraculous end to his father Guy Gibbs' five-year housework hiatus, a sheetless night is on the cards tonight. Frankie's unproductive, leisurely bedroom-bound night on the piss all but guarantees that no washing was done. He strips the sheets off his bed so roughly that it shreds down the seam. About time one would say, given its ancient cult status within the family after being passed through two generations. But with a three week wait until his next universal credit payment, and left down to one currently dirty sheet, it could not have happened at a worse time.

Frankie forcefully wraps the manky sheets into a ball and heads authoritatively for the bathroom. A door downstairs clatters and he freezes in the hallway – the location of many septic foot wounds caused by pointing nails sticking out of the uneven floorboard. Nobody comes up the stairs, all clear for now. He storms for the bathroom. Off come the damp pyjamas, but his trousers, seemingly glued to his legs, prove far from a breeze to rip off. Stuffed in head first with all of his might, the dirty laundry initially fits in the washing basket. Once Frankie collapses onto the shower cubicle floor, it slowly expands to the point of hanging out of the open lid, dripping with piss and sweat. He stuffs his head into his hands as tears trail between his fingers. An unnerving racket from the disastrously unsafe shower fitting – that's at least ten years overdue for replacing – ensures his anonymity in the paper thin-walled terraced house where most is heard between rooms. Horizontal fresh razor wounds on his right shoulder partially open up and ooze out a touch of blood.

Metres away down in the living room, Frankie's long-time friend Alfie Fenner stands leaning his elbow on an enormous snooker cue case. Caked in Dax wax, with slicked back hair and a smart grey suit jacket, he's way out of place in these most unglamorous of surroundings. The presentability of which isn't helped by the unofficial house servant's self-imposed night off on the piss. Guy's stain-ridden high vis jacket – sported at last night's heavy pound-a-pint session down at the local – is of stark contrast and befitting to the houses disarray. His supervisor role on a building site, which he's casually two hours late for today, allows him the privilege of washing it as he feels. Guy's youngest son Dazzler makes the most of his teacher shortage enforced half school day by gloomily pursuing Premier League and European glory with Liverpool on Fifa career mode. An epic challenge given his recent ascent in game difficulty up to legendary.

"Space with us, should you be after some proper match practice!" Guy proposes.

"Full squad I thought?" Alfie dismissively mutters.

"I'll sack any of the ten journeyman fucks on the squad off, any of them!" Guy passionately declares in his desperation to sign Alfie – an elite player at local level – up for the pool team that he captains.

"Tuck tuck, all fucking night! All you past it never had it mugs do." Alfie mockingly imitates the delicate type of shot required for tucking someone up.

"You haven't a scooby of our impenetrable dominance in the Bangor league."

"Maybe if the standard was in the slightest bit stimulating."

With respect to the Bangor pool league, its standard proves a stimulating challenge to those outside of the sport's professional ranks. Boasting a plethora of international and county level players, its one frame shoot-out format ensures a challenge for any player to remain unbeaten over an entire twenty match season. Fearing his reputation as a budding professional snooker player will bring out the best in his opponents, Alfie finds it safer to pretend he's above that level.

"Div one champions last year Fenner boy, I'll have you know," Guy proudly says, reminding Alfie of the pinnacle of his eleven years as captain.

"Not just on about the pool though am I, rammed full of janky munters that club of yours."

"No way! More student pussy down there on a Wednesday than you could fucking fathom."

Indeed it is a hot spot for *student pussy*. Not that Guy stands even the slightest chance of pulling a single one of them, which consecutive calamitous failed attempts has

8

proven. Despite the fortune of a relatively handsome face and strapping physique, Alfie's dearth of pulling power, subsequent inferiority complex, and anger towards women has lately developed into a baseline curiosity in the incel community.

"Oh right yeah, let's say it is. Why then is it you skulk off to Vietnam, fucking flower seeking." Alfie jabs Guy in the crotch with his cue case. "That grubby little chode of yours senseless, for your entire month of paid holiday, every bastard year?"

Guy's vigour diminishes, all but crushed by the damning summary of his rigid optimization of leisure and free time. "Yeah well, that's not all I do out there is it?" Other than the hotel's two-star hygiene rated kitchen's all-you-can-eat buffet, where he stocks up on energy for the following day's conquests, it is.

"Won't mind taking Dazzler with you then?" Alfie optimistically asks.

Guy shudders at the mere thought. Brothels that know him on first name terms, narrowed down to his favourite three that he rotates for daily visits on his trips, wouldn't let the boy through the front door, not like the unregulated good old days.

"Fearful all the birds will have me instead," Dazzler sarcastically chimes in, without taking his eyes off a crucial

Fifa EFL cup semifinal clash with Huddersfield, that he holds a slender one nil lead in.

Deep down, Guy knows his womanizing peak was over at nineteen after putting on four pounds of flab following a futile attempt to quit his half gram a day cocaine habit.

"D'you think the other reason I piss off for is?" Guy says.

Alfie fails miserably to restrain the urge to groan. "Frankie stuck here babysitting again!"

That puts any late night best of nineteen frame slogs, an inevitable ten nil win for Alfie more often than not, out of the question for an entire month. Not just any month, but the last month of practice before his first pop at snooker's Q school – a gruelling tournament held once a year, the only gateway into the professional ranks. Should he pull Q school off against the odds, it has been assumed that Frankie will serve as his semi willing full-time practice partner. A decision in itself that puts Alfie's slim chances of sustained success in peril given Frankie's comparatively lackluster ability.

"If he fucking knows what's healthy for him." Guy fiercely chugs down a grainy, lukewarm cup of tea. His incessant partying means babysitting, along with 'unhealthy' mental and physical consequences for the few times Frankie's dared defy or abandon these duties, have been a recurring theme of his eldest son's free time.

"Come on Gibbo, you'd have been all over that!" Alfie picks up and admires a square framed hung up picture of Guy's rough, pension age, simple-minded father holding a two-foot carp by an angling lake. "Grubby old Gibbo senior, and your pleasant self out there shagging in grotty little brothels when you were a squirm? Character building shit, that Dazzler's set to miss out on."

Frankie cuts Alfie off by bursting in. Alfie and Guy smirk at each other, both sensing Frankie's sleep-deprived, agitated entrance leaves one of his vast array of trigger points wide open for exploitation.

"Oi oi." Guy nudges Alfie's shoulder with his elbow. "Only that sodding mardy when he's pissed through last of his bedding."

Dazzler turns back to his game. While perhaps prone until recently of joining in with the bullying, by now he's nearly broken out of seeking Guy's fatherly approval. No longer does he blindly follow Guy's despicable treatment of those weaker than him. Even at the age of twelve, he possesses enough empathy to sympathize with the never-ending barrage of unanswered grief that flows Frankie's way left, right, and centre. Frankie heads for the cupboards, determined not to gift them the satisfaction of reacting. He deliberates between the cupboard's sole two choices of cereal, Asda value frosted flakes, or unsealed stale porridge oats, before eventually settling on the former.

While bracing to pour out a bowls worth, Alfie glances over. "Oh mate no time for any of that cardboard drivel." He struts over and snatches the box out of Frankie's hand. "Old school Ken's opening up three hours early, missing Bethesda's cricket div four title decider, just for me. Unprecedented I'm told."

Be sure that it is, never will a more ardent fan of Bethesda cricket club exist. Cricket season Saturday mornings are usually a write off. As his loyal, habitual late-morning pint guzzlers – who miss out on at least four precious morning drinking hours at their beloved sanctuary – will attest to. Even if the customary forty-six missed calls left by his regulars, all diligently waiting outside the club on fold up deck chairs, does occasionally coerce Ken into skipping his traditional post match pint with team captain John Bâch.

"Head's all over the shop Alf," Frankie sheepishly claims while rolling a fag to avoid eye contact. Not a surprise considering their eight consecutive days of six-hour snooker sessions.

"And what?" Alfie quivers, taken aback by the prospect of playing on his little lonesome once again, something he can't stand for longer than forty-five minutes.

"Not got what it takes today I'm afraid."

"Bailing on me, just before fucking Q school." Alfie gazes away into the distance with manipulative in-authenticity.

"Last fifteen days I've been down there with you." Frankie heads for the door while tucking up his fag.

"Oh this languid little dolestar isn't bailing, lying round my house all day! Telling you now," Guy militantly bellows, sticking his stiff, stumpy arm out and halting Frankie in his tracks.

"Wouldn't be on the dole had you not tormented my fucking supervisor, calling him a Paki and that, would I?" Frankie says with every bit of resentment the subsequent nine months of scraping away on Universal Credit has bunged up.

"Fucking forgot my double meat! Thieving prick deserved more ask me, Paki or not. You don't want to be working with people like that anyway."

What Guy crucially leaves out is that he did get 'more'. In the tune of following the bloke down a mountain path and knocking him out cold from behind, with a knuckle duster no less, leaving him needing a metal plate jammed in his cheek. This satisfied Guy's need for justice, but not nearly as much the hero's acclaim thrown his way by his mates. All had been falsely led to believe Guy did the poor bastard in for shafting Frankie short of half his wages.

So off they wonder for yet another snooker session. Electing for the scenic route on this occasion, Alfie tears through a sparsely populated, sleepy, mountainous village four hundred metres above sea level. He rags hard on the revs, being sure to let the ever-suffering villagers know of his acquired on finance, brand spanking new Honda's recently installed hair dryer sounding exhaust. This is a significant detour, and a doubly unusual choice for someone as stingy as Alfie, or 'energy efficient' as he puts it when called out. Alfie reckons the pre-match mountainous stimulation depletes Frankie of energy. This couldn't be further from the truth as he slumps in the passenger seat devouring a paper thin fag – or as Alfie would call it, a 'jail rolly' – taking no notice of the scenery he's desensitized to and takes for granted.

"Be me and you on the road after I turn pro." Alfie proudly winks at Frankie, who pays him no attention.

Once Alfie's focus switches firmly back onto the road, Frankie rolls his eyes subtly out of sight. Despite knowing Alfie's a terrific player, one of Gwynedd's all-time best, he holds brittle faith in his slender chances of making it as a pro and providing employment.

"Professional ball racker, free tickets to my games. Shits all over a stab at Subway management!" Alfie gazes optimistically at Frankie and is disappointed at failing to extract any of the expected titillation out of him.

A stab at management is an understatement. Possessing all the competency and social skills required for a promotion and having devoted three years to the place, Guy's bi-daily racism-filled visits were the only thing standing in his way.

"Chance for you to finally provide for Dazzler. Not long now," Alfie sharply adds with a tinge of resentment at being ignored.

Got him, a deep thud on a selection of Frankie's nerves, preying on the downside of his subsequent two years of unemployment that brings him the most insecurity and shame.

Frankie momentarily glares at Alfie without being spotted. "A life changing opportunity for me, no doubt." His sarcasm is only marginally picked up by Alfie. He goes in for a hefty toke on his skinny, half smoked roll up as it burns down to within millimetres of the filter.

"Made us that rolly then, or what?"

Frankie checks his tobacco pouches meagre remnants and sighs. "On pure dust over here man."

"Come on mate. Left mine at home again didn't I? Only a fucking rolly."

What's Frankie's is to be shared in Alfie's eyes, and he feels thoroughly entitled to deliberately leave his tobacco at home and pinch Frankie's. This is partly in passive aggressive punishment for Frankie having never learnt to drive, leaving Alfie to take them everywhere. Frankie flicks his fag stump out of the window, tears open his cutters choice pouch and pours the sandy dust remains into a rizla.

After a pit stop insisted on by Frankie to the village corner shop, who still remarkably sell Urban tobacco for one pound

15

fifty per five grams despite the new thirty gram minimum law, they arrive at the unassuming, unsigned mock Tudor style snooker club. Alfie bursts out of the car, grabs his rigor mortis dog's coffin sized cue case and looks the place up and down, lapping it all in as if arriving to play at the crucible theatre itself. They scrape their scalps on the borderline illegally short door frame as they enter the unremarkable, dull bar setting – something Old School Ken holds no desire to improve upon. The place's customer demographic of old men couldn't care less about anything other than the nineties-era pricing of pints remaining intact. A selection of them duly lap up this cherished opportunity for late morning pints in their fiercely protected, self-designated square foot spots their stools simply have to occupy. While the punters pay no attention to the lads as they enter, Old School Ken nods half-heartedly their way while softly mopping the floor near the dart board. A job he despises, and resents his long-term cleaner – who's on maternity leave after the birth of her seventh child – for leaving him to do. A pint of Worthingtons and a double gin with ice sit on the bar awaiting them, as there customarily is at bang on Alfie's regimented 10AM daily arrival.

They trundle up the narrow windy stairs towards the dimmed-out snooker room; Frankie in front, of course, to serve as a beta walker for the constant puddles that form from the crumbling roof's many leaks. Alfie beams gleefully at the sight of the empty room. With the pick of the tables available, he heads straight for the renowned match table with an eerie dark purple cover. This table's special to Alfie, having watched Ricky Walden play an exhibition on it when he was ten – saving three months pocket money up for the privilege. Despite holding bitter regret for failing to get his autograph as hoped, this still remains the highlight of Alfie's childhood. He pirouettes unnecessarily around the coin metre controlling the table's light and theatrically drops a pound in it. A meagre twelve minutes is all that provides. Despite being the instigator of the sessions, it's Alfie's mission to contribute as minimally financially to them as possible. This is made possible without detection by Frankie's nonchalant habit of placing his entire session's budget on top of the machine. So being non the wiser, Alfie pretends to put his own money in while Frankie isn't looking.

As per his unspoken duties, Frankie folds the thick, heavy table cover to the impeccably tidy standard demanded by the die-hard league regulars, who use the table for league snooker. Alfie meanwhile, sands down his cue tip. Once it's primed for action, he whips out his elite level gleaming box of snooker balls, all proudly polished the night before, and passes them to Frankie to set them up. Alfie believes Frankie needs all the practice possible ahead of his inevitable future career as his assistant. Once the balls are set, Frankie lays two cue balls on the baulk line for the lag –

the single simultaneous shot that decides who breaks. This is based on whoever's ball lands closest to the top end after hitting the bottom first. As usual, Alfie waits for Frankie to hit his shot first, which ends up being inch perfect, nestling tightly on the top end of the table. Defeated by Frankie's unexpected excellence, Alfie doesn't bother hitting his. Frankie gives Alfie the nod to break.

"Fuck sake," Alfie mutters under his breath, resenting the fact Frankie would have pelted his and left him a long-distance sighter at the very least.

Such is his vexation, Alfie forgets his customary chalking of the skin between his thumb and second finger and slams the cue ball down between the brown and green ball. While still taking his usual care with the shot, racking the cue back and forth ten or so times, he smacks it with excess top spin. This sends the cue ball smashing into the pack of reds, flying in and out of the baulk area, leaving it nestled next to the blue with a smattering of loose reds open. This uncharacteristic error on Alfie's part leaves Frankie with a few sitters for his opening red, piss easy for someone of his ability. A sitter it is, yet Frankie makes a total meal of it, miscuing the shot rashly but still managing to pot the easy straight red. Excess top spin however, sticks the cue ball tight on the bottom right side cushion, leaving him an acute angle to pot the black ball – the only colour readily available. His already gloomy face dours. While being a competent potter, his concentration often lets him down when trying to compile breaks over thirty. Not on this occasion, in which the black ball flies dead into the middle of the pocket. Alfie's face enviously sinks as he swigs his gin and reluctantly re-spots the black ball, as is the etiquette with snooker. Buoyant from the excellent shot – a one in ten usual chance of nailing both pot and position as he did – Frankie gets down for the next shot and smacks in the straight mid-range red without touching the pocket's jaws. Such is the stun on the cue ball, it leaves him perfectly on an easy pink, that he duly sinks without thinking twice, barely adjusting his body position to do so. Alfie begrudgingly re-spots the pink, although ever so slightly off its spot as to try and gain any sort of advantage possible. Instead of sitting back down, Alfie lingers around the table, waits for the exact moment Frankie cues up his next shot, glides slowly past and fiddles with the pocket's net. Frankie scuffs his shot, as Alfie knew even the slightest of distractions would incite.

"Buckets my arse," Frankie grunts, disputing Alfie's insistence that the tables here have gaping pockets.

"Frankie Gibbs, fifteen," Alfie announces in his nearly perfected snooker referee tone.

Frankie roughly shoves the shabby club cue into the corner, slumps into one of the fifties-style deep-seated armchairs and chugs the remaining half of his pint. Frankie's custom Riley's three-piece snooker cue, that had set him back a pretty £99.99, among his all time priciest purchases, was deliberately left by Alfie at the dodgy local boozer on a pound a pint Wednesday. He'd known full well it would get nicked, and that Frankie's performances would suffer by using Old School Ken's shoddy club cues.

Alfie gets down mischievously on his opening red and smashes in the mid-range pot with excessive top spin. "GET me a gin and rocks," he says while remaining in his shooting position with his head turned back in Frankie's direction.

Frankie painstakingly checks his wallet and pulls out the last twenty pound note of his monthly universal credit allowance. It's by no means beyond Alfie to get the drinks in, especially considering his full-time job selling sanitary products in the dingy local nightclub's bathroom. However, he takes pleasure in depleting Frankie of his funds, always keeping a mental note of the lad's precise current wealth. In spite of this coming out of his food shopping budget, Frankie gets the drinks in without question, fearing an earful of self-pitying manipulative guilt trips otherwise. Something like how Alfie *'always pays for the petrol',* and gets them discounted snooker sessions through the landlord's dream of being able to claim a pro trains at his gaff. Or his favourite: that Frankie would have been *'bored shitless'* in the house without the opportunity of a snooker session, and that one round of drinks is nothing as a way of showing the requisite gratitude for that.

On the frames go in their traditional first to ten match. Unable to recover from the sheer agony of his first shot, Frankie performs poorly, miles off his usual standard. Alfie wins the first, with a break of forty-seven being enough to seal it. Frame two and three swiftly follow in similarly domineering fashion as Frankie necks pint after pint, relegated to slumping in his seat and re-spotting colours. A customary ten nil win is soon upon them. Alfie's half arsed day's work is done, with far gnarlier tests awaiting him at Q school tomorrow.

After leaving Old School Ken a fifty pence tip each on the bar, post-snooker excursion nosh is the only thing for it. There will be no debate as to grubby old Mike's Bites serving as the location for this escapade – a diner on upper Bangor's mid motorway outskirts, caked in eighties themed upholstery that beams out a semi-impressive neon shop sign. It's Alfie's all time favourite establishment hands down, and as such, there's never a glint of compromise on the subject. With Alfie having made sure Frankie will be skint by the time they get there, all the bargaining power lies with him given that he'll be picking up the tab; little does Frankie know, from an allowance his mother dishes out before snooker for the post-session grub. Not, as he'll undoubtedly claim as a future guilt trip, from his *hard-earned wages*.

They perch themselves down near the rusty, chipped paint back door leading out to the joint's dull concrete yard, with Frankie's back to the bustling traffic of people streaming in and out. It's Alfie's table of choice for two reasons. Firstly, because those heading out for a smoke will see his chode of a cue case, thus in his eyes, expanding his sporting profile. Secondly, because people brushing past non-stop makes Frankie somewhat uncomfortable. Alfie's already sipping his double gin and tonic, ordered free of charge by texting the place's doting young waitress, who's infatuated by Alfie under the illusion he's already a pro snooker player.

"Nothing like those midlands academies to get match sharp boy. You saw it first-hand today," Alfie coolly claims, snugly lounged back on a cushioned seat.

"So did you give old Shaun Murphy a lesson on the baize then or what?" Frankie asks with beady interest.

"Fat bastard didn't give me the chance." Alfie looks down at the tatty plastic table linen.

"After all that jib he were dishing you!"

"Basically all the lads were there, you know, Dominic Dale, Kyren Wilson, even the thunder from down under rocked up." Alfie hits his thumb against his fingers in between assertively rattling each name off.

"Money matches again I assume?"

"Round robin mate! Couple of grand each, the porcupine prick did just edge me out." Alfie's eyes whirl around as he struggles to think of what to say next.

"Oh no shame in that mate," Frankie reassuringly says after an awkward pause.

"Didn't matter! Basically, I slaughtered Dominic Dale, got a century, then annihilated the Warrior. Dale was loving it, rolling over table the lot! Ended up calling me the warrior, basically stole Wilson's name. It was quality."

"Brama that is mate, just wish I could have been there!" Frankie taps his beer bottle against Alfie's.

"Best thing is, Shaun Murphy didn't even turn up!"

"No-show prick, after all that."

"No-show prick sticks to his home table whenever One Visit's in town boy."

A gaunt, ragged-looking waiter rocking an uneven, sideburn-prominent stubble and sideways fringe hairstyle subtly appears, hovering by the table while holding two menus. His unassuming presence leads to him being entirely unnoticed. Alfie eventually spots him, grimaces his way, snatches the menu and vaguely flicks through.

"Bacon cheese burger, all the salad and chips," Alfie says, without looking the waiter's way, who scribbles down the request with shabby, graffiti-style handwriting.

"Right, I'll--" Frankie stutters.

"Oh and a tuna spud while you're at it." Alfie cuts Frankie off and holds out his menu, impatiently inviting the slapped arse faced waiter to take it back.

Their waiter turns to face Frankie with a shallow grin.

"Errr, fucking, fry up please mate." Frankie drops the menu on the table after his uncharacteristic decision not to copy Alfie's order.

Our waiter darts to another table, disappointing many others glaring his way who are long awaiting the only waiter on shift's service. Frankie's hand quivers delicately. Alfie's open mouthed, despairing glare beaming his way as of the split second he placed his order spells trouble.

"What on earth are you on? Fucking fry up?" Alfie intensely asks.

"Didn't have chance to scran my bastard cereal did I?" Frankie confidently responds, hiding his paralyzing fear of Alfie's disapproval.

"What kind of FREAK has a beer with a fry up?" Alfie shrieks, his sense of tradition and expectation that everyone follows it boils over. Frankie shrugs and takes a decent chug of beer, droplets fall from either side of his mouth due to his shaky hand. "Take another swig of that and I ain't paying for the order!"

Frankie continues to swig his beer, finding a level of assertiveness ordinarily alien to him.

"Least a five mile trek down the fifty-five from here bert," Alfie warns.

With Mike's Bites being conveniently slap bang in the middle of a semi-newly built dual carriage way running through North Wales, Frankie's trek back would be hazardous to say the least. He slumps back in his seat.

"Not like you've got any dough on you is it?" Alfie's focus quickly returns to the bottle of Hobgoblin. He grunts and emphatically ogles the beer. "I just can't hack this monstrosity."

Alfie grabs the bottle out of Frankie's outstretched hand and pours it out of the back door, much to the shock of the surrounding tables. That is other than a couple of fat, hairy bikers purely absorbed in the entertainment unfolding in front of them. An elderly Mike's Bites stalwart on a nearby table – disgusted that his precious bacon bap and morning bottle of Stella dared be disturbed – glares at the waiter. He ponders intervening before scuttling off and wiping down a table facing the opposite direction. As the Hobgoblin gold slithers down the asphalt backyard, a brown Cane Corso dog tied up outside gratefully licks up the unexpected treat flowing their way.

Chapter 2 - CEX roadtrip (Flashback)

A pungent stench, one Frankie had grown to loathe even by his tender age of eleven. Be over though, once it's sent slithering down the sink hole, for now. Well worth being on the thick end of a slap for, but chances of that were likely anyway. Whether the wine – a stomach-churning thirteen percent Pinot Grigio on this occasion - went down the sink hole or his volatile mother's trap. At least this way his *day* – which had become a rough two-day sleepless stint owing to barmy cocaine parties hosted downstairs by his parents – might stand a fighting chance. This five-in-the-morning-desperation-derived experiment was a true stab into the unknown: how would Joss Gibbs fare for three days without wine? An irresistible opportunity for Frankie to find out, especially given the painstaking week of whinging about being skint until payday. Even from Frankie's financially naïve perspective, he struggled to buy it. Buy that a thoroughly respected mental health assessor – the county's senior decision maker as to who's referred for mental health care, and who is paid double the local average salary for the privilege – could ever find themselves in such a financial state. It didn't cross his mind for long, as the blame surely lied with his idle, semi-retired-at-thirty-five construction site manager father for having two years off work. Phantom anxiety and depression diagnoses being his excuse, complaints Frankie had heard him bragging about fooling multiple doctors into signing him off on.

First bottle down. The stench was almost enough to make Frankie quit, but he couldn't give up that easily. He tossed the green-tinted bottle aside and delicately opened the kitchen's outdated, seventies-style cupboard doors. It's difficult to say what troubled him most, two crusty slices of mouldy bread being the cupboard's solitary food content, or the sight of three further unopened bottles of wine. A daunting few minutes of that ghastly aroma lied ahead before it's mission accomplished. Not one to shirk a challenge, he cracked on despite the hunger pains growing by the second, made worse by knowing they wouldn't be cured anytime soon. In the bin the bread went first of all, with Frankie taking no chances. Despite it being what most would deem undoubtedly past its edible state, it was far from inconceivable that his father Guy would use it. If he could use gone-off meat in a similar condition on the sly, chopping around the mouldy bits, bread is far from off limits. Especially with a steaming hangover stopping him wobbling three hundred metres down to the local bakery for something fresh. Last night's serotonin-sapping excursions meant he'd probably be in bed by bakery closing time, heightening these chances. Bottle by bottle, Frankie tipped the wine down the sink, millimetres away from puking down his faded hand-me-down t-shirt by the time he's on the second. He only managed to avoid this through closing his eyes and thinking of every crucial upcoming West Ham. Having recently figured out the world of online streaming, he would be able to watch every last one. Devastatingly, the plethora of pop-up ads and a lack of internet confidence had limited his football intake to Match of the Day to this point. That is other than when invited over to the technologically sophisticated Fenner household for dinner and a sleepover with his chum Alfie.

BANG! Out of nowhere came a smack on the back of the head from Frankie's sleep-deprived mother Joss, snapping him out of jollier thoughts in an instant as he dropped the bottle in the sink. Joss desperately reached out to grab it, with her other hand throttling the back of Frankie's neck. *Too late.* All but empty. Her snarling glare descended into despair, her eyes whirled in all directions, pondering a way out of this withdrawal-ridden three-day nightmare now on the cards. Her small group of addiction-riddled friends would no doubt be too skint to bum a lend off. Pound a pint and the scattering of preying cocaine dealers waiting there to pounce on that four-pint-deep loss of inhibition eats up their money. Inordinate amounts of subtle one-drink-at-a time lends over the years, despite being the highest earner of the group, meant her credit was up many moons ago bar to buy food for the kids. A lie Joss had spouted, and would again for twenty quid's worth of cheap rosé and amnesia haze.

Joss gazed back at Frankie, wishing he'd never been born. "Things I must've done in a past life to have an ungrateful fucking DINGBAT like you squeezed out of me ey?"

Frankie hung his head in shame and gazed down at his abnormally large feet. Teasing dished out about his *'clown feet'* at football training the day before only amplified the inescapable disgust that swarmed through his soul.

"Ey?" Joss slapped him across the cheek with an open palm.

Her slaps never usually came in bunches, so a real threat was now present for Frankie. Up his hands went, mimicking an orthodox defensive boxing stance learnt from Fight Night Round 3. Not that he was as scared shitless as his stance made out, but he had a gut feeling that should another punch come flying his way, it'd be with closed fists. Then anything was possible. Her violent outburst of last month and the stint of consequent concussion and dizziness from his burst ear drum still lived vividly in his memory. While being a match for most men and a solid puncher who usually aimed for the temple, Joss had loose accuracy and was still half asleep. One of her swingers could easily land square on the ear, and another week stripped bare of football training was not worth risking.

"I don't like how you are on the wine!" Frankie sheepishly forced out.

Joss scoffed dismissively, her extensive, strenuous efforts to stifle Frankie's bravery unraveled in front of her desperate eyes. She bent forward patronizingly with a wry smirk.

"Should have taken you to fucking rot in care."

"Nothing stopping you!"

Bang! Barely having left Frankie time to finish his outburst, Joss walloped him flush on the jaw, her fist well and truly closed this time. Frankie stumbled back, open mouthed, clenching his brutalized face.

"Where despicable little shits like you belong." Joss wickedly cackled. "But I'd be looked down upon, even if everyone knew what unforgivable bother and bedlam YOU bring to this family! That is what's stopping me." She slammed a pile of paper off a nearby table. "Now fuck off upstairs, and get your telly!"

"No! Please, please I won't do it again, ever!"

"And your PlayStation and all. NOW! You're coming with me, to trade the lot in." Joss dragged Frankie away by his t-shirt, his knees painfully scraped on the thick, rough brown carpet. "We don't get enough to replace the wine, then back for your second telly we'll come."

Which is no isolated threat, the difference being this time that Frankie is actually being told, albeit violently, rather than his precious gear being carted off while blissfully unaware at school. Without doubt, the charming young oik donning the CEX checkout would throw a bit extra onto the trade in prices, naïve hope that Joss would finally accept one of his creepily persistent invitations for a night on the lash being why. They were quite the trade-in regulars there, selling various household electronics, with the majority being Frankie's. Although Joss's tried and tested Comet television scam of deliberately and subtly breaking a new flat screen, taking it back, and getting three new TVs on store credit consistently ensured Frankie wouldn't be without one for long. Be an average of a month until the guilt of her actions overcame his witch mother.

Chapter 3 - On the supermans

Early evening winter darkness is upon them as Alfie slowly pulls up outside the Gibbs' family house with a brimming grin of content slapped on his face, fuelled by the mounds of energy extracted from Frankie all day. A flickering lamppost luminates their detached terraced house and the front garden's scattering of stray rusty car parts salvaged from construction sites sitting on the scabby lawn. Frankie sinks deep into the passenger seat as he picks up the blare of self-righteous sniggering, broken drunk chatter and heavy generic house music bellowing out of the place.

"Another grot-infested night for you in paradise squire." Alfie peers towards the open window and grins wickedly. "Gibbo's got his number one munters round."

"Wouldn't go near the caveman," Frankie claims, a fact that's stood the test of many pathetic attempts by his father.

Sally and Stacey are anything but 'his munters', given Guy's nine-year sex drought bar paying for the privilege. Alfie's one of the only drips in the tiny city of Bangor to believe such fibs. Others are either shit scared to, or not interested enough to challenge his delusion of alpha male dominance over his friend group, who see Guy's role as a party host and not much more.

Out steps Byron Wee wee, emerging gracefully through the stratosphere of duty-free fag smoke and stale, amphetamine-induced sweat. His ridiculed name dragged through a generation, bestowed upon him after his chronic house burglar of a father pissed his pants before his inaugural court appearance. Being a local small bag drug dealer, there's no doubt why he's about. Despite not following in his father's footsteps categorically, the piss poor purity of his drugs have routinely had him referred to as a *bank robber* by customers. His baggy, non-fitting, roughed-up dark blue tracksuit bottoms scrape on the soft, muddy grass.

"Byron Wee wee the lot. Best mates you and him ain't you?" Alfie grimaces, thinking back to his primary school-aged rivalry shared with Byron over feeble old Frankie's attention and devotion, a battle Alfie eventually won after an inordinate amount of effort.

Byron belatedly spots the car and squares over, his vacant gaze lights up at the prospect of more swift potential business. "All right lads!" He wiggles his hand in a rock and roll, Dio inspired second and fifth finger pointed up gesture.

"Get out." Alfie revs his engine to the max.

"What?" Frankie eventually replies, still stoned out of his mind after a cheeky half gram spliff Alfie made in a lay-by on the way home.

"Get out my fucking motor. I'm not having that froogy anywhere near me!" Alfie's urgency deepens with every step closer Byron takes. Frankie leisurely opens the door and looks around for any left belongings. "GET OUT!" Alfie shoves Frankie out and hurtles off, slamming the door shut from the inside as he speeds off, leaving Frankie sprawled out on the lawn to get up and dust himself off.

"How are ya' square tyre!" Byron offers his hand out for a shake. Frankie looks down and elects to fist bump him back.

"Yeah sound mate. On parole early then, once again?" Frankie unconvincingly quivers.

"Course I am. Your old man and his wreck-head buddies have afforded me quite the cushty existence since."

"Have they yeah?"

Despite Byron's drugs being of a notoriously shoddy standard, they are passable by the majority and get somewhat of a job done. What Byron does bring to the table, that keeps him in the game, are competitive prices, unmatched outside of the big-time bulk sellers that are well out of local recreational users' reach. Frankie knows his father and mates will all be selling bits of speed and cocaine after Byron's visit. This ensures their own personal stuff is free, meaning longer and more frequent parties at his house. Byron continues rattling off barely impressive statistics and milestones of his post release earnings. None of which Frankie takes any notice of, with his mind firmly on the sleepless nights and carnage ahead. Both of which will entail the chugging of at least four pints to stand the slightest of chances of sleeping through. They part ways after an awkward handshake-turned-fist bump, and Frankie skulks inside to face his fate, slamming the front door behind him.

Guy's joined inside by his old mates Pedr Ogwen, Razza and Pedr's long-term on and off partner Stacey. A fiery, promiscuous sort whose had countless affairs behind his back. Notwithstanding this, Pedr remains trusting of her, putting up with it partly out of inescapable fear that he's punching above his weight and couldn't dream of doing better. Completing the sweaty line-up is Stacey's unassuming best mate Sally, a reluctant member of the group who only stuck around for access to cheap drugs. Her ever-increasing cocaine habit's slowly blinkering the reality of her sheer lack of similarities with any of them.

Three quarter-ounce cling film-wrapped bags of weed sit on the table being communally chain smoked – one so carelessly placed on the edge of the table, that a bud or two slides off every time it's picked at. A promising result for Frankie or Dazzler tomorrow, both standing to profit from the sloppiness of others in floor lemon kush. Pedr chomps half of a superman MDMA pill and puts the other half back in a communal bag of twenty on the table. While weed and MDMA gets this lot tingling, it's not nearly enough to sustain the night. Their main squeeze is undoubtedly cocaine, of

35

which plenty is flying around too. Guy crushes up a gram's worth on the same piece of granite he's owned since the age of nineteen. This stuff however, is closer to the category of bash, which, as the name suggests, is bashed up with benzocaine, vitamin B, or some other cheap mixer.

"Oh and that Barry Hawkins, bald cunt, cost me a brick load earlier," Guy says, ruefully alluding to a squandered four hundred quid staked on his lunch break down at William Hill.

"I've told you once." Razza dabs a chunk of cocaine onto his gum with his thumb. "And I'll tell you again mate, you are a fucking spastic for not getting on the cryptos with me."

"Oh fuck all that dross bert. Nah, nah, at least if I blow my dough down the bookies, straight back into the British economy," Guy emphatically responds with his typical British nationalist intensity.

Razza pauses and stares vacantly at Guy. His entire savings and leisure time out of work going on holidays to Asia surely means he's being ironic, but not a flicker of that possibility presents itself. While Guy's ready to continue this farcical argument, Razza scoffs and snatches the granite tray boasting a tasty selection of slug lines, snorting the non-chopped-up one. Guy gasps and Razza winces and wrings out his head. A nasty rock in the line that not even his semi-functioning left nostril can handle eventually flows through his airways after a brief scare. Frankie apprehensively sneaks in, desperately attempting to remain undetected, which quickly proves unsuccessful. A mostly positive, welcoming collective drunken roar erupts at the sight of his presence.

"How are you lad?" Pedr slurs, leaning back and holding his hand out for Frankie to slap.

"Oh, I'm sound me," Frankie says.

Wanting minimal exposure to the dishevelment unravelling in front of him, Frankie briskly heads into the kitchen.

"Bollocked any of those Tinder birds yet or what? Who was that troll, what was her fucking name." Guy's drug-fried memory briefly fails him once again. "Kes!" He bursts out, a discovery made after using Frankie's phone without permission to order a takeaway. A lifetime ban slapped on him by the town's sole two kebab shops for racially abusing staff mean he can't use his own. "Tidy little sort. If that's your thing."

"What you on about bollocked?" Stacey asks, her tone as sincere as her repulsion.

"Got to put something in her ain't he, that's what blokes like him do, all in." Guy bursts out in laughter that's met by cool silence amongst the room.

Frankie scoffs at the joke commonly thrown out at his expense and reaches all the way to the back of the dam under sink cupboard. A four pack of pint sized Kronenberg cans are conveniently hidden in a hole behind a multi-pack of toilet brushes – a deliberate tactic to deter Guy from ever finding them.

Vague, gloomy late morning winter sunlight pokes through the half-shut curtains and showers the sheer turmoil left in Guy's wake. Empty bottles dripping out runny ash after being used as makeshift ashtrays and a dried blood stain from Pedr's torrential nosebleed are noteworthy. Some of the blood trickled onto Dazzler's beloved Xbox and Fifa case. Broken glass, flaccid balloons, and a scattering of nos canisters add to the dreary checklist of chores Frankie's day will inevitably be dominated by. Most surprisingly of all, plates and makeshift DVD cases harbouring crumbs of cocaine lie everywhere. Uncharacteristic wastefulness, with it not being typical of the group to leave such valuable resources in their wake. Perhaps a signal of their newfound collective jackpot in Byron Wee wee and his cheap, accessible gear. A result for Guy, now having tasty treats galore to kickstart his faltering mind upon awakening. Spilt curry takeaway curiously occupies all corners of the room – a sure sign the cocaine was weak, as a curry would ordinarily be unfathomable if they were as wired off the stuff as desired.

Frankie stumbles in with a pounding head courtesy of yet another hangover, made worse by the paper thin one-pop joint he's toking. His torn, baggy tracky bottoms flap around his ankles. Stale sweat and alcohol fumes lumber up his airway and the chore-ridden day ahead stares him square in the face. In preparation, he cracks open a window and tightly shuts the curtains carelessly left open. A shattered bottle of Jack Daniels Fire with a footprint blood trail leading out of the room swipes his attention. Fearing the worst, he launches his fag into one of the array of ashtrays. He is led by the blood trail to their dingy, outdated downstairs bathroom – a place littered with the most hideous fittings the seventies had to offer, only made uglier by the selection of varying coloured vomit interspersed around the toilet. To Frankie's horror, Dazzler's sitting upright in the bath, wincing with steely determination in his eye and his hands perilously close to a piece of glass lodged in his foot, sticking out half an inch.

"Don't touch it no!" Frankie yanks Dazzler's arm safely away from the glass.

"Not keeping it in there for footy am I?" Dazzler says, deadly serious about making it to a crucial school team practice, the last before their crunch tie with feisty rivals Dyffryn Ogwen.

Frankie carefully examines the damage and shakes his head. "Jammed right in there that. We're going A&E, come on."

"No fucking way!" Dazzler squirms backwards at the thought.

"State on that Daz!" They share an intense stare off before Frankie scowls and dials Klaus Cabs' number. "I'm belling a taxi, and when it gets here, you're fucking getting in it."

"You heard what social services said last time!" Dazzler belts out. "A&E will be all over that."

Frankie looks down at his feet apprehensively, coy over whether to hang up the call with it being Guy's last chance at holding custody of Dazzler. His grip on keeping this dire environment for a child under wraps – a skill taught in depth by his civil servant ex-wife – has waned as of late. As such, neighbours have submitted a catalogue of complaints, expressing significant concern about Dazzler's safety.

"I don't want to be any more of a tramp than I already am."

Enough's enough, no little brother of his is rotting away in the system. Frankie storms out into the living room and whacks out the infamous miscellaneous medical box. Its dreary, murky colour, rough outer plastic interior, and creaky hinges just some of the signs it wasn't a twenty-first-century purchase. Inside is a healthy stock of thirty milligram Valium and Zapien mixed pills and a few strips of ten milligram Valiums. Not what he's after, but a mental note worth making for next time Sir John Benzo's needed to help cure any

40

insomnia. Instead, he grabs a roll of bandages and a rusty pair of tweezers, quickly dispelling any qualms and assuring himself there's no other way out of this predicament.

After scrambling around for anything close to disinfectant without luck, his eyes clap onto a half bottle of cheap, nasty Lidl vodka. A king-sized Frankie Lampard senior poster on the wall gives him the kick up the arse needed to get it done. He trickles some vodka onto the tweezers while strutting out of the room. In the short walk to the bathroom, his nerves and inner voice wreak havoc on his newfound confidence. All the times of being told his co-ordination was *'dog shit'*, his lack of connection and trust in himself, the lot. But it's time to step up, with failure to do so having never bared dicier consequences. Frankie sheepishly bumbles back into the bathroom and places the equipment for the job down on the surface. Swiftly acknowledging the level of its filth, he takes the tools back off.

"Oh won't be on the shorts today me," Dazzler grimaces. "Should've seen Jonny on the Kovosier last night!"

"Oh aye?" Frankie says with dwindling focus on what's being said as he scrubs the filthy bathroom surface with disposable wipes.

"Hanging out of his arse he'll be."

"And how did you get all that?" Frankie belatedly switches on to the ludicroucy.

"Some creep, fucking, Damo his name was. He went in for us. Only asked for three bar!" Dazzler says, proud of him and the lads' success getting booze from the shop on their first crack.

"Must be raking it in then."

"Jonny got at least half a bottle down him man." Dazzler bursts out laughing. "Currents on the Menai Straights nearly took him clean down to Dublin! Four of us had to grab him. Always said, fair play to him, boys, my thirteenth aye, is gonna' be fucking out of this world! And he didn't half deliver." His smirk's soon wiped as Frankie slumps over the side of the bath with the Vodka.

"Be grim this for a sec." Frankie dangles the vodka, steadies his trembling hand, yanks hold of Dazzler's ankle before dripping barely a shot's worth over the shard.

Dazzler instinctively kicks upwards with his other foot, avoiding the planting of a shiner on Frankie by a whisker courtesy of slick head movement.

"Not quite the mad man you make out," Frankie says.

"Just, just do what you got to do. I'll keep still." Dazzler shuts his eyes.

Frankie peeks closely at the glass, anxiously hesitating before sticking his head into the danger zone of Dazzler's leg space. "Shard's barely poking out."

Frankie peers up full of dread and shuffles out into the kitchen, facilitating an eerie silence for Dazzler to ponder what is to come. Following a twenty-four-hour pre-drinking session at the family house, prior to their parents inconspicuously darting off to watch Primal Scream headline Gottwood festival, Dazzler suffered a similar fate at the hands of stray sesh glass at age four. With no one about, and having been strongly advised never to phone ambulances or police without permission, a bit of Google research taught Frankie to heat a glass bottle to get it out. That time, the shard was half the size, and Frankie's far from the happy-go-lucky, confident lad he was then. Unfortunately, on this occasion, there isn't a three hundred and thirty milliliter bottle in sight, the ideal size for the job as it leaves less air to fill. Forced to settle for a six hundred-and-sixty-milliliter Heineken guzzler, he dabs the bottle tip on a preheated electric hob. About a minute usually does it. He taps his index finger on the thing to make sure it's up to task, which a surface burn confirms. Despite having worked at Subway and been subjected to countless toaster burns and lectures on post burn procedures from half arsed middle management, he rinses his finger under the cold water. Without hesitation he storms back over to Dazzler and places the sizzling bottle tip over the shard.

"Hurts you fucking prick!" Dazzler screams and flails his legs about.

Frankie yanks the bottle away. "Daily ring sting from Bryn Y Neuadd grub, one out of five hygiene rating, worst care home in the country is gonna' sting a hell of a lot more."

Dazzler holds his head back, resigned to his fate and within seconds comes the sweet clanging of the shard shooting out of his foot.

Frankie swivels the bottle around, exhibiting the fruits of his heroics. "No brother of mine rots away in Bryn Y Neuadd."

Without giving the soppiness of his deceleration time to set in, Frankie dollops a chunk of the vodka on the open wound, inflicting pain piercing beyond belief, worse than the extraction itself. He then laps it up in shaky, borderline vintage bandaging.

"Not exactly what you want before school aye?" Dazzler jokes as he's lifted out of the bath and struggles to reach the door without limping.

"Out of all the days you actually want to go in?"

"Got Syr Huw down their place! Captain today. But I'll get the sack if I don't go in every day this week. From the team, and possibly the school." Dazzler sighs. "Lard arse social worker cunt won't think twice about doing Gibbo!" Dazzler looks down shamefully at his bloody socks. "And to add to proceedings, my last pair of socks they were."

Frankie nods and heads for his sock draw, concealing the disappointment of his sock collection of three pairs bearing one clean pair left at a push. An examination of the draws confirms his suspicions – one measly pair of worn-down grey socks, threatening to burst out in holes at their next challenge of durability. But there's no choice and he lobs them at Dazzler. Frankie can't help but giggle as Dazzler slips on the ill-fitting socks as they droop over his feet like a baggy condom. This stops as Dazzler struggles to stick his shoe on, a feat the progressive swelling is making harder by the minute. Frankie carefully helps slip the shoe on.

"Can't even do you a taxi," Frankie mutters with his face blushing red raw.

"Ten-minute shit on the bog, and train's free! And if they catch me, I'll just pretend I'm a mong." Dazzler drags his foot on the floor as he walks out of the door.

Frankie stares vacantly into space, taking in the harrowing DIY operation and bracing himself for the hours of laborious house work ahead of him. To help, on goes King Tubby, an all-time dub favourite of his. After an eternity perched down on his stiff hip sweeping every last shard from under the sofa with a dustpan and brush, it's on to the bathroom. An explosion of varied-coloured dried vomit, some of which spewed up with no effort made of getting it down the toilet awaits him. After a quick splash with the shower head to finish off the scrubbing, the room's spick and span. After unsuccessfully mopping the latest permanent spilt ashtray stain on the linen and five trips out to the bins with stacked bags of bottles, Frankie spots a bud of weed on the floor. A result. He puts it safely aside for a tasty late morning leveller. Last but not least are the cocaine plates and cases. Any thought of Dazzler snooping a pop at the free drug remnants lying about, as he occasionally does, doesn't bear considering. Frankie thoroughly scrubs them down and leaves the glistening plates drying on the airer.

Finally, he can flop out for this long-awaited joint. This time a tasty bit of skunk dropped by Razza, stuff pined over so desperately that he hides it to avoid being heckled and guilt tripped all night for not sharing. Understandable enough, with his mates left languishing in the dull high of Byron Wee wee's shabby mass-produced county line farm weed. Half a gram at least Frankie reckons, maybe closer to a gram given its density. He grinds the lot up and his renowned rolling speed puts the joint together in no time, albeit regrettably with flimsy tobacco dust from the end of a BHS pouch also salvaged during the clear-up. Guy stumbles through the door in his classic grubby white vest and black Adidas joggers. Sweat spews from his pours as he waltzes in with a manic jig to his step while clicking his fingers and belting out the chorus of 'Bed's Too Big Without You' by The Police with appalling rhythm. All is *seemingly* well as he wonders into the kitchen in his own world. Still pissed as a fart and shaky, he fills up a kettle in the kitchen, but fumbles it into the sink as the wind's thumped out of him by the sight of the gleaming row of chaotically stacked plates airing out. "Shit a brick, ain't sterilized all the plates have you boy?" Guy desperately asks.

Panic stations set in. An amateur mistake, the worst thing Frankie could've done, leaving Guy unable to guzzle the collective crumbs to sooth his grittier than average comedowns. Frankie gets up to leave, not up for hacking the inevitable grief coming his way. A penetrating slam from the next room stops him dead in his tracks. Three vintage Japanese plates shatter on the floor, collapsing the awkwardly stacked pile. Frankie swiftly pockets his phone and tobacco pouch and stumps out his long-awaited joint.

"Get here a minute will you squire, fucking rinsed to be clearing this up!" Guy shouts from the kitchen.

"Going dole," Frankie says.

"It's dicey for Dazzler like this," Guy sternly adds in a manipulative guilt trip-style tone he saves for special occasions.

Frankie recognizes this but can't prevent the gouging of his buttons and stops en route to the door.

"Wait there, wait there will you." Guy deviously scuttles over holding a quarter full bottle of vodka by its neck, smirking insincerely. "Just wanted to say, how splendid it is it see you, see you seshing, getting on it, having a right mad one!" Guy chugs some vodka before holding up the bottle and frowning at its dwindled remains.

"Used a bit," Frankie confidently claims.

Guy's ferocious glare knocks the stuffing out of him.

"Had to disinfect Dazzler's sliced up foot," Frankie adds far less convincingly.

Guy lightly nods, his bloodshot eyes remain fixated on Frankie.

"Swear down! Believe me, I wouldn't go near that utter garbage for a laugh."

"Alcy liar! Just like your cheap slag of a mother was!" Guy sticks the bottle into Frankie's cheek. "Come near anything I bought, that I earnt, you idle cunt, and I'll shatter this, or something just as sharp right in your fucking mug," Guy says with cockney pronunciation learnt from his adolescent days spent trying to be a hard nut in farmland Kent. He turns Frankie around and boots him hard on the arse.

Frankie clatters forward into the door, catching the side of his head on the corner of the letterbox.

"I'm the only one who works in this house!" Guy insists.

Guy threateningly braces himself with the bottle of vodka and hurtles it Frankie's way. Frankie only just manages to slide past the stiff door as the bottle shatters all over it. Some of the glass escapes outside through the diminishing gap as the door's shut.

"Fuck do you think you are!" As Guy struts into the living room, he turns back to the door. "Tell the dole office you're an 'orrible selfish rotter while you're out there boy!"

Suddenly overcome by a destabilising dizziness, he collapses onto the sofa. Right in his eyesight is Frankie's bonus spliff reluctantly left only moments earlier, which he sparks with his trusty pink clipper. Taking in an ambitious first drag given his declining lung capacity knocks him for six. He wretches out in a desperate coughing fit before a dreaded reflux gag sends shock waves through his senses. Anticipating his fate, he sprints to the bathroom, dry heaving the whole way.

Chapter 4 – Brama (Flashback)

Frankie's eyes abruptly burst open. No doubt the odds-on favourite at 5/6 had to be the criminally unstable hand-me-down IKEA draw set and the three-day-old crusty Coco Pops bowl shaking vigorously on top. But one could not rule out the screeching drunken roar that echoed through the floorboards from downstairs. What had woken Frankie up this time? On this occasion at least, it wasn't romping in the room next door. All were issues usually reserved for the minds of most undergraduate students living in halls, not eleven-year-old boys like Frankie. If he ever got there himself, he'd be well-versed in that life. A hybrid of eighties techno and hard style mercilessly shrieked through the speaker downstairs having been turned up, muffled arguing added to the chorus. Frankie's clammy head jolted up. He chucked his West Ham covered duvet on the floor and sprinted into the bedroom next door, solely focused on the safety of his three-year-old brother Dazzler.

When it was evident that Dazzler was fast asleep and seemingly safe, he gasped a hefty sigh of relief. What had caught Frankie's attention more was the sheer mess of his poor brother's room. A modest number of toys and teddies sat scattered around on the floor. Among them, a Blue and

Grey Beyblade that laid shattered to bits. To make matters worse however, left carelessly in the corner of the room was a used condom, a smashed bottle of rosé wine, and four cigarette butts. A clear indicator the room had been made good use of during one of Frankie and Dazzler's commonly enforced sleepovers with ill-fitting babysitter families, that both boys loathed spending time with. Within the civilized world, never would that have been considered an acceptable space for a young child to sleep. As was becoming the norm, Frankie made a mental note to clear the tip in the rapidly approaching morning – one of the many domestic pressures unfairly bestowed upon him.

After trudging back into his own room, Frankie sank into his scabby office chair. Its cheap plastic cover was intact, but torn to shreds, as if its previous owner had anxiously pinched it nonstop. A feasible theory, given the stressful and erratic nature of running the under-performing 'Cube' Nightclub it was left outside of. Foam poked in out in parts, which made it rough on your arse or sleeveless arm. Frankie didn't mind whatsoever, with it being his first proper chair. Despite its condition, there wasn't a shred of doubt in his mind that the time and energy spent lugging it half a mile down the high street was worth it – even with his parents' utmost efforts to convince him otherwise. No longer did he have to lie on his springy mattress with pathetically thin pillows propped up against the wilted bed board to watch telly, nor play his beloved PlayStation 2 from a strenuous distance for his undiagnosed long-distance vision issues.

A devilish-sounding hard house tune by 2050 rippled from the speaker downstairs, one of the rigid selection of tunes that played on repeat whenever Guy hosted seshes. Frankie sarcastically tilted his head back, bobbed along, and swivelled left to right in his chair. He checked the clock on his left, which read 4.58 AM, 4.45 if you accounted for the clock being set forward. Frankie's lingering fear of being late ensured the clocks were always ahead, a fear driven by his mother's sheer impatience and awkwardness when it came to anything Frankie liked doing. After two gruelling years of begging to attend Bethesda's football practices – the only local team – Joss had finally agreed to drive the seven-mile round trip lift each way. However, Frankie dared be ready one minute past Joss's deadline of 6.45. As punishment, she refused to entertain the idea of a lift again, to anything that didn't serve her in some way. With Frankie strictly forbidden from riding alone by bus, this indirectly banished his chances of playing competitive football and diminished his only other avenue out of the madhouse, bar school. 4.45 AM would usually be Frankie's ideal wake-up time, leaving a cushty four hours before dreaded school to get right into some PlayStation. This time was usually split two hours each between FIFA career mode and his beloved Tekken 3, before throwing on his creased uniform and bolting it out for the 8.50 AM school bus. This also acted as a distraction from hunger, since neither of his parents ate breakfast and, as per their single-minded parenting style, didn't expect anyone else would need to either. A blockage to the downstairs toilet meant today was different, with his usual dawn vibrancy scuppered by the casual flow of party guests inconsiderately stumbling up for the upstairs toilet, tarnishing Frankie's chances of deep sleep. But with no choice in the matter and slim chances of getting back to sleep for a rare 6 AM lie in, Frankie wheeled the chair over to his bright cream-coloured desk. From the desk, he grabbed a filthy miniature round glass ashtray with six spliff ends inside. To Frankie's delight, one of them was chunky and only a third smoked – as fat a joint as Frankie would have smoked in his brief smoking career. Must've had his room shagged in and all. Any invasion of privacy Frankie felt was entirely cancelled out by the thrill of being guaranteed to be nice and wrecked before school. That's if he decided to go in at all, which on party nights like this was generally left down to him, as Guy and Joss tended to pass out until 2 PM.

Out came the trusty stale stenched scissors to chop the ends off the tasty spliffs, a trick learnt by spying on his father when he ran out fags. Chopping them off gave the finished product a far superior taste, Frankie had found. Any harshness from smoking this way had long stopped bothering him. Five of the smaller spliff ends' combined remnants, when chopped open, provided what could only be described as a dusting to supplement the contents of the chunkier joint. With the king skin bulging full, it proved a rolling challenge and a half for Frankie, needing fierce concentration to successfully tuck the rizla. Although a hand-me-down, Frankie couldn't have been happier. His very own fat spliff, all to himself! He took the time stroking over its baggy, unrefined exterior, examining every angle of it. He took out a jet lighter and a standard, safety-less disposable with a broken flint, and used the spark to genie the other. A bulging four-inch flame burst up, startling him and annihilating the tip of the joint, side-burning a quarter of the thing. Nevertheless, Frankie basked in his cheddar, haze and skunk combination head high. So much so, that it was fifteen minutes and three heavy tokes spread out by eyebrow-threatening excursions with the dangerous lighter until Tekken 3 was summoned. Having recently obliterated his all-time record of staying unbeaten on Tekken ball for three days straight, Frankie relished the chance to extend this as soon as possible. Just two more days to beat the school bully Mo Spud's highly disputed claim of having lasted a remarkable six days over daily five-hour sessions unbeaten. With this being the same dude who claimed to have shagged three teachers, one of them twice, the Tekken Ball school record most likely belonged to Frankie already. But the competitive animal in him was keen to avoid any doubt. Little did Frankie know until thrusting open the empty case that this wouldn't be possible. To his horror, he peeked up at a gap where the console would ordinarily be. What a disaster; he easily pictured its precise location down on the high street's grubby little GAME branch. Or maybe CEX, on full display, awaiting some lucky little bastard to have it bought as third choice console off their soft touch parents for Christmas. Despite the family's supposed detrimental lack of finance – that Frankie had been made more than aware – there happened to be a roaring party downstairs, all surely bankrolled by pawning out his prized possession for the third time this year. With his head firmly pressed into his hands and his whole body shaking in disgust, he lit the joint back up, singeing his eyebrow with the genied lighter yet again.

There was only one thing for it. A sweet spot existed on the farthest side of the landing that, if jumped up and down on, would be heard by all, no matter where they were. A spot far enough away from all rooms that Frankie would have time to leg it away and escape a clouting. Although an infrequent tactic utilized by Frankie these days, it felt like more than a fitting punishment for their part in his non-gaming morning, let alone a barren Christmas holiday. A form of terrorism not utilized since its prominent employment before he turned seven. At which point, he had just figured out how to make the most basic forms of breakfast, no longer needing to wake them up to eat anymore. With the

Tekken case in hand, Frankie stomped up and down, shrieking with every bit of melodrama his malnourished body could muster.

Pedr and Razza were sprawled out at the bottom of the stairs on a grotty, springy double mattress. Being without sheets or bedding, and subject to the unavoidable blaring of tunes from the next room, it was difficult to fathom how Pedr managed to even half doze off. Something Razza, despite being initially optimistic, realized was increasingly unrealistic for himself when adding Frankie's tantrum into the equation. Wearing a tight, pink Fred Perry short sleeved polo shirt and camo pattern shorts was not his wisest decision. Previous Gibbs' house parties ending with damp sleeping conditions should have taught him that. Not that he had much choice, having promised his wife Linda that his cocaine days were over. A short stint in prison during the early days of their relationship for dealing cocaine, and the subsequent heartache suffered in his absence, meant they would be finished should she find out. Work meetings with the national rail lads in Liverpool was the fib of choice, aided by another fib that he'd been promoted to Railway Supervising Engineer two years prior. When in reality, remaining a basic level engineer that was never invited to work bashes. A precarious lie that one bit of semi-thorough familial financial analysis from Linda would shatter – a miracle that given her invasive nature hadn't yet occurred.

Pedr alongside him was having the nicer time of the two, despite barely passing as conscious. His round, bald head bobbed from side to side with the music as he laid with a fat grin on his chops. Arguably, his comfort under the circumstances could have been attributed to his far wiser clothing choice of trusty Adidas black and white joggers and a 3XL sized, tucked-in, long-sleeved Hawaiian geometric shirt. However, it was hard to ignore the avalanche of drugs and alcohol in his system. Pints with Razza from 1 PM down the social club after a half day were inevitable. Pedr despised his plastering job with a passion, but spent too much money getting wrecked – namely on Valium and Hobgoblin ale – to risk jeopardizing it. It all became too much for Razza as he groaned and, with all the energy that remained in his body, turned over to Pedr.

"Pedr lad," Razza muttered. Pedr's eyes opened, but words failed to flow naturally out his mouth. "Going to have to ask you to part with a generous chunk of them Vallys I'm afraid." Razza stretched out his hand.

Pedr tried and failed to sit up, crumbling pathetically into the wall, his neck nestled jaggedly, facing Razza with a disorganized smirk. His pupils had retreated so far into the back his head, you'd have to question if their return was a given.

"I'm brama me." Pedr says in his native Bethesda boy version of an English accent.

"Well I'm pretty far from fucking brama in every measurable regard here mate." Razza mumbled while he sat up. His back arched forward as he rubbed his face, somewhat gathering his disorientated senses. His teeth ground together, both due to his low body temperature and the speed-cut cocaine still parading through his veins. "Not all of us had a year-long T break and get as wrecked as you!"

Pedr's year off the drugs following a rehab trip funded by his wealthy parents had indeed crashed his tolerance, especially when it came to Valium and weed. Frankie's attention-seeking rang through Razza's ears, becoming increasingly irritating. Although he had always had some guilty empathy towards him and Dazzler, he heavily enabled and indirectly encouraged a lot of the children's neglect at the hands of their wreck-head parents. They'd partied as a group together since the nineties, four-day-long hard style raves were their bread and butter. But these sort of house parties were as good as it got for them by this point.

"Ahh Pedr Ogwen man!" Razza rubbed his throbbing sinuses. "Don't be a prick for once, Gibbo's kidders on one now the lot."

With his flickering eyes barely opened, Pedr attempted to swipe the Valium packet over with his hand, only moving them a matter of inches.

"Get 'em down you then you pansy." Pedr slithered further down the wall, wedging himself awkwardly.

"Dingler." Razza reached over and grabbed the packet.

Although having no issues subtracting the first two pills, the tricky third proved troublesome, especially for a supposedly seasoned sesher like Razza. Anticipation for the soothing relief he'd soon be overcome by hit hard. Without hesitation he shoved all three Valium down his trap. It soon dawned on him that he had nothing to chug them down with, crucial with these dark web-acquired Valiums Pedr sought out in bulk.

'No one in 'Pesda knew what hit them' Pedr had boasted upon their first spell of circulation eighteen months prior.

Problem being, their above average width made them tougher to swallow. Three simultaneously was pushing your luck. Using a stale, half-drunk can of Kronenberg next to Pedr, Razza chugged the whole lot. Something he wouldn't have dared consider before turning twenty-five, and would have berated anyone in his presence for doing. An old mucker from his school days perished on his sixteenth, having mixed one ten milligram Tramadol and a couple of cans of beer. However, this principle had become obsolete before long, graduating to him eventually peer-pressuring others into doing so.

Out of nowhere Frankie stampeded around the corner, leaped onto the top step and ran down, clearing two steps at a time, not initially noticing Razza and Pedr's corpse-like existence at the bottom. Razza choking up his pills in shock scuppered their anonymity. A scramble on the mattress ensued, with Razza paranoid about Frankie clapping his eyes on the pills and losing the sensible role model uncle image he naively thought he held – a key source of his narcissistic supply. Given the Valium tolerance Razza had, the two remaining in Pedr's strip wouldn't even touch the sides of his craving, adding to the importance of finding these.

"Frankie! Iawn washi," Pedr muffled with barely open eyes.

With the Tekken game case in hand and toking his makeshift joint, Frankie glared suspiciously at the pair before strutting into the living room. Multiple marginally full bottles of spirits and spilt cans of beer contributed to a ghastly stale odour Frankie's nose was privy to. Five lines of cocaine remained on a piece of granite next to a rolled up fifty-pound note, a new discovery for the boy. As neglectful as his parents were, they'd always done a top job hiding the sight of hard drugs other than weed away up until that point. Lying with his legs bent inwards on the sofa, Guy snored dangerously hoarsely. Seven cigars inhaled like normal cigarettes that night were to blame. Frankie trod his bare foot in a puddle of beer and ash and shook it, grossed out by the cold tingle that shot through his body.

Quickly, his attention flickered over to Joss lying vertically by the foot of the sofa, vomit down her top and a trickle of dried blood on her nose. He screamed and legged it over. "Mum?!" He shook her by the shoulders, to no avail. He shouted in Guy's face from a distance. "Dad! Mum's in proper trouble!"

Guy grunted, his legs jolted and his eyes flickered. "Scuttle off you rotter."

"Dad! She's not moving!"

"I'll make you breakfast IN A MINUTE." Guy snapped his legs out, still half asleep and energy-sapped by his dopamine deficit.

Frankie slapped Guy across the face with the Tekken 3 games case and copped a punch back from Guy's lying position, sending Frankie flying backwards a few metres.

Guy jumped up and scowled. "What have I fucking told you about coming in here while our mates are over boy!"

Guy reached for a lighter, only then, to his horror, noticing Joss on the floor. He checked Joss's non-beating pulse and let out a deep and eerie yelp. Razza burst in and spotted Frankie on the floor crying.

"Razz. Fuck sake mate, she's choked it, out for the count. Well and proper," Guy said, blubbering into his hands.

Razza collapsed to his knees, while Frankie stopped crying, got up and stared blankly at Guy standing over Joss's body.

Razza assertively picked Frankie up, covered his eyes and carried him out. "Get up there, and look after your brother. DO NOT come down until you're told," he warned, leaning down in the corridor.

Razza slammed the door behind him, but it bounced back open, affording Frankie a cheeky view into the room, which he duly gazed into and watched the pair pacing around.

"Help us stash all the gear before we call it in will you?" Guy pitifully asked Razza.

"Fucking right, I ain't getting sent down again." Razza cleared incriminating evidence into a carrier bag chaotically.

Guy spotted Frankie staring in, yet glared back menacingly, which freaked Frankie out as much as anything in the whole sequence of events. Razza charged towards him, frothing with rage. Frankie dashed up the stairs, tripping on the middle step.

"Get the fuck upstairs, NOW!"

Chapter 5 - Getting fit for black mirror

Dazzler perches mischievously by the dull, outdated train station waiting room's vending machine while Jonny scopes the place out for any sniff of a weakness. His rough upbringing in the care system has dished him out quite the entrepreneurial outlook on life – a prominent factor as to him and Dazzler's lifelong compatibility. His thick glasses and gawky appearance act as the perfect foil for an otherwise unassuming schemer. Wilder is far less enthusiastic and sits on his arse, leaving the graft to those two. His oversized Thrasher jacket and blonde curly mop of hair epitomize the dishevelled developing punk rocker look he's yet to fully master.

Jonny spots his chance in Cowley, an overweight, ginger-haired, grey-suited company man throwing abuse at the vending machine. From extensive analysis of the machine over time, he knows the top right hand corner cog is liable to malfunction. In the very cog a bottle of Lucozade orange dangles delicately, having not left the machine following payment.

"Oh!" Cowley pathetically slaps the machine, with nowhere near the requisite power to get what's rightfully his. Another two quid and a button press later, he erupts after accidentally selecting an empty cog, clenches his fists and storms off. "Train station fucking scam again!"

Without thinking twice, Dazzler skips the hysterical belly laughter immobilizing the others and bashes his shoulder into the vending machine's side.

"Go on Daz! Pretend it's Gibbo lad!" Jonny chants.

After a few unsuccessful bashes, Jonny and Dazzler turn to the nonchalant Wilder, grab an arm of his each and with no objection from Wilder, hurtle him into the vending machine from a few feet away. Four bottles clatter out. They celebrate their haul-for-the-ages wildly and sprint onto the train with Wilder taking two of the bottles, an unspoken rule for whoever puts their neck on the line.

"All that for an original man!" Jonny bitterly remarks.

With all possessing a glorious view from their train table, Cowley reappears alongside a quivering train station attendant half his size. Realizing his beloved dangling Lucozade has vanished, he slams a chair into the vending machine. Jonny shakes up his bottle and lobs it through the closing train doors, nailing Cowley square on the head.

"Wheey! Wobble off ginger prick." Jonny gives Cowley the middle finger.

"Enjoy your porridge in the morning lad." Dazzler sarcastically waves at the powerless Cowley.

Following a pit stop in the toilet conveniently timed as the conductor checks tickets, the boys strut off the train. All are pleasantly proud of their free train ride and drink to start their morning. Especially as its vacated the capital to chip in on a thirty-gram pouch of Sterling. Dazzler's heart sinks, having never seen a soul manning the Bangor train station barriers until this moment.

"Shit boys." Dazzler scampers out of his view. "Barrier dick."

Jonny and Wilder head forward with little sympathy, safe in the knowledge their caregivers leave just about enough aside for them to avoid such situations.

"Do us that rolly then." Jonny stealthily tries to nab Wilder's pouch.

"Fucking scav man." Wilder dangles the pouch out of Jonny's reach.

"You owe us one from last night!" Jonny insists, impressively recalling such minute detail in spite of being flat out paralytic.

Fearing the unbearable tit for tat should he not oblige, Wilder reluctantly hands over his pouch as they tap their tickets on the barrier.

Dazzler stumbles towards the barriers alone, exaggerating his limp. "Hello sir. Had a little bit of a fall on route, has caused quite the torrid episode of immobility," he says in a believable, well-spoken southern accent. "Ticket must've..." Dazzler rustles through his pockets.

Without so much as a peek his way, the brute, impassive guard scans Dazzler through the barriers. Wasting no time, Dazzler struts though, fucking off his exaggerated limp. Low winter sunlight obscures his view of Jonny and Wilder making skinny roll ups by the entrance.

Frankie sits back lethargically in the deliberately soulless job centre waiting room for his weekly appointment, surrounded by a wall full of job notices printed in tacky old word art, as exciting as the menial jobs advertised on them. With a bent posture befitting of his reluctance to be there, he scours through the Sun newspaper's football pull out. A rare treat given that no reading material other than that local job-seeking-related is usually provided. A shock that the trusty staff – who are devoted to authoritarian shepherding into work – will have something to say about when they realize. Sully, a stocky lout bursts out of the appointment room door to Frankie's shock, red-faced and seething.

"How can you even contemplate sanctioning me?" Sully says, pointing into the office.

"You know how it goes." Colin coldly shrugs his shoulders, well and truly living up to the nickname *sack lunch Col*. A name gifted to him based off an inexplicably high sanction rate in comparison to rival job coaches, and the subsequent skipped meals of the many who've faced cruel financial hardship at his hands.

"Yeah what leave your old man for dead, just to come fucking dole?" Sully shouts, his fists clenching ever tighter by the second having witnessed his father suffer a near fatal seizure days prior, following an all-nighter on cocaine and Valium.

"Nothing I can do," Colin condescendingly says.

"You literally would, wouldn't you. John Bâch, conked out on your floor, fifty years of 10 AM jars down wethers with the boys, finally catches up with him. And you'd fucking leave him there! To come here! Not a shadow of a doubt."

"I've belled security, so you better be on your way really." Colin's upper lip trembles at the mere reminder of his cruel father's alcoholism, a moment of weakness he'll kick himself for while watching the EFL highlights tonight.

"Nah nah, fuck that," Sully says. Two short and stubby security guards, both dwarfed by Sully, grab an arm of his each. Sully bats them both away. "Get your filthy hands off me. I'll fucking have you," Sully claims right in the larger guard's face. Sully walks away unassisted and quickly turns back. "You know I didn't dodge that appointment, rotten as they come, fucking rat bags like you!" Sully shouts as security wrestle him out of the office.

"You've had your hissy fit-- now piss off!" The smaller guard barks out.

"Get off me now!" Sully swats them both away and raises his fist. "I know where you live you meatball cunt." Sully squares off unassisted, both nervy guards linger behind him from a distance.

Undeterred by the commotion and in no mood to fall behind schedule, Colin sticks his head out of the office with an undeniably stern glare. "Frankie Gibbs." He ushers Frankie in with his index finger. "You know why you're here yeah?" Colin asks, barely giving Frankie a chance to sit down on the stiff blue chair opposite.

Frankie sheepishly shrugs as he perches himself down on the very edge of the seat.

Colin grunts. "Maccy D'z have been belling me flat out, telling me their new star pupil, don't wanna' know."

"I thought I told them, and you--" Frankie fearfully answers while gazing down at his battered shoes.

"E? You know what this means aye?"

Frankie stays glued to his shoes, knowing fully well the type of form that Colin pulls out without having to look at it.

"When we give you graft, and you sack it off because you can't be arsed, you've got the clap, your ferret's got a blister or whatever the fuck it is."

"I - I couldn't do those hours," Frankie mutters.

68

"Now, you tried to have that one on with the last cunt you saw here." Colin passes over the sanction form. "Ninety-one-day sanction. High level, okay?"

"Have to look after my brother at night. Can't be leaving him there alone."

"While Gibbo's his legal guardian and you're on the dole, having been so for over a fucking year, you'll do what we say or this is only the start for you."

Jonny, Dazzler and Wilder giddily form a circle in a part of the school field perfectly arched as to hide their passing round of Wilder's last cigarette for two pulls each. A fag that, based on usual playground rates of thirty pence a roll up, has a market value of at least a pound. One that could have been stretched out into a few, but as per Jonny's opportunism, he rolled it into a cigar-sized smoke, not knowing where and when his next nicotine hit may come from. A bustling fifteen-a-side football game takes place behind them as two popular female students spot them and head over.

"Oi oi," Jonny chants as he notices. His nerdy looks mean attention from females his way has been minimal so far, with smoking becoming somewhat of a gateway for him despite his pathetic flirtation game. He grabs the fag out of Wilder's mouth and passes it to one the girls.

Dazzler shoots off, acknowledging his chances of another drag have hit zilch. A ball Is pelted his way and he enters the game by pirouetting around a fully kitted kid and around another with a stepover. Still somewhat pissed off at his last fag having been given away, Wilder sprints up to Dazzler and executes a robust but fair sliding tackle, one befitting of his status as the year's top centre half. Dazzler clatters to the ground. A few sympathetic classmates gather around, but most quickly crack back on with the game.

"Iesgo banol dâd be ti di neu' troma?" Shouts the suave deputy head teacher Dinorwig, fresh from a cigar break in the back seat of his brand-new Mercedes. He jogs over, undoubtedly restricted by his tight-fitting light blue tuxedo jacket.

"Dwi'n iawn!" Dazzler desperately yelps. He forces himself up and sprints away out of the school gates, heavily limping yet still comfortably evading Dinorwig.

Now, the brisk few-minute walk to the train station with a now-aggravated limp was bearable, and it was unlikely the school cared enough to chase after him. While he'd been threatened outright with expulsion, dwindling pupil numbers, and Dazzler's average potential grades with the right application ensures this outdated joke of a school will again let this misdemeanor slide. At worst, they'll throw a detention his way that neither pupil or teacher bothers to turn up for. Besides, even if they did make an example of him, the thought of being caught with that negligent-parenting-inflicted injury and the care-home-sized consequences aren't worth considering.

Disastrously, an older, sterner-looking chief was donning the barriers this time around. A new recruit that, having been made redundant from his trucking job of thirty years, has a point to prove in relation to his working competency, throwing a spanner in the works for Dazzler. After an unsuccessful sprightly scout around for possible loose tickets on the floor, he lumbers away defeated, with the day's events having diminished his never-say-die opportunism.

Whether his father's vintage Volkswagen Scirocco had been written off in the months prior or not, the chances of a lift home are non-existent on the best of days, leaving him facing a four-mile trek down country lanes and main roads. After climbing an excruciatingly steep and long hill, Dazzler faces a painful stretch of road swamped so heavily by wilting, barely living trees that the beaming sunlight struggles to poke through. A paper-thin road wide enough for one car to squeeze through, separated by a shallow ditch with thorny wild blackberry bushes either side. A hundred metres deep in, with no room to turn back, a green Lamborghini tractor bolts up. Rhys josc's behind the wheel, a careless, drink-driving inbred, an unsavoury character conceived by prominent local farmer Kev Iorwerth and his cousin. Their family nickname josc is based on their stereotypical farming attire and attitudes, a shortened version of the word joscin. Dazzler buries himself into the spiky bushes as the tractor narrowly squeezes by. Rhys honks his horn and merrily raises his thumb at Dazzler, who doesn't acknowledge him back.

A grizzly long stretch of pavement-less dual carriage way awaits him after, leaving Dazzler to chance it down the grassy bank full of ankle-deep muddy bogs. He rolls up his now torn up school jumper sleeves and winces as they catch a fresh thin cut inflicted by one of the larger brambles. A police car hurtles down the empty road, slowing down as it passes Dazzler. Its snarling driver Gavin cunningly peers his way before speeding off into the distance. Dazzler rips off his school jumper and pelts it into the bushes, not that the town's lax coppers are overly bothered by school truants, unless they're shagging one of the teachers. Back round the cop car creeps, this time scampering at a walking pace alongside Dazzler.

"How are you Dazzler?" Gavin asks with a seedy lack of authenticity that only contributes to negative police stereotypes. Dazzler marches forward, paying no attention to the coppers. "Trek from here lad. Couple of hours, at the very least."

"Getting fit for black mirror me. Only chance I'll ever get rich, on them bikes you'll be putting us on soon," Dazzler claims, having had his view on authority skewed beyond his family's natural anti-establishment culture even further by watching all of 'Black Mirror' at a young age. A programme he genuinely believes was released in order to get us all ready for the crash of civilization.

While Gavin's clueless to the reference, having sworn against ever getting a streaming service in favour of keeping faith with the trusty old Freesat box, his partner Gwyn cackles. His heavy weed habit having given him similar paranoid thoughts, especially after smoking skunk seized from scouse county line dealer kids flogging it around the pier.

"Might as well jump in chief. We're off that way anyway! Natter with your old man," Gavin cheerfully says.

Dazzler phlegms towards the car door, narrowly missing it.

"Wouldn't want the birds seeing you hobble round like a mug," Gwyn reminds him.

An observation that stops Dazzler in his tracks. After a brief dalliance of reluctant deliberation, he gets in the car and slumps sullenly on the back seat. He takes a first real look at Gwyn, a rookie policeman in his probationary period. In small areas like this, the personnel of bobbies on the beat is a hot subject, and given Dazzler's early forays into shoplifting, it's only wise he gets to know what he's dealing with. Bangor's newest slouches out on the passenger seat,

73

sipping from a disposable Starbucks cup, sporting a flamboyant eighties-style copper moustache with no other facial hair and tinted sunglasses. A style proportionately out-of-place, down to his lack of believable conviction in the look and unimposing aura. Dazzler's hangover and dehydration from the tough walk causes him a moment of dizziness as he scopes Gwyn out.

"Hanging out your arse you lad," Gavin says.

"What?" Dazzler defensively replies.

"Been on the jars with the old man have you?" Gwyn patronizingly asks.

Dazzler peeks out the window, refusing to be drawn into any mind games. Gavin smirks at Gwyn, both relishing the opportunity of making the son of one of the local force's most loathed individuals uncomfortable.

"Reckons he's too good to be around us he does!" Gavin resentfully says.

"Yeah, all these crazy seshes we keep hearing about, does an invite ever come our way? Does it fuck," Gwyn flamboyantly adds.

"Not what I'd consider a fitting environment for a--" Gavin peers back at Dazzler, momentarily taking his eye off the road. "School-aged child."

"You haven't been near a fucking party since your mam sliced your caterpillar cake on your sweet sixteenth and let you lick the knife, chief," Dazzler boldly responds.

Gwyn erupts in laughter mid-coffee-sip, spitting it out over the dashboard. Gavin tensely grips the steering wheel and grits his teeth. His party drought has in fact spanned many years, all the way back to his older sister's eighteenth where his invite was more out of sympathy. He rips the seal off a pack of ten menthol Sterling Cigarillos, sticks one in his mouth the wrong way around and lights it, only realizing after the first toke.

"What are you doing?" Gwyn judgmentally asks, slow to realize Gavin's smoking.

"Chuck us a few over and I'm grand. Won't hear no more of it," Dazzler proposes.

"Pull over you fucking loony bin!" Gwyn snaps his fingers in Gavin's face.

"He said he's all right!" Gavin restlessly says.

Having had an alcoholic father who burned through fifty a day – with the vast majority of them their diddy council flat's four rooms they shared between them – this plays on Gwyn's conscience. Especially given the resentment held towards his father for indirectly starting his own nicotine addiction aged eleven. He slams Radio Cymru on, slamming the volume up and down from zero to a hundred repeatedly. A Mark Drakeford speech about second home owners flooding local first-time buyers out of the areas mortgage market screams out of the stereo. With Gavin continuing to toke on his harsh cigarillo, Gwyn takes the drastic action of reaching over and flickering the cars sirens on and off. Gavin ultimately gives in, slams on the breaks, pulls into a lay-by and storms out of the car to the side of the road. Sensing an opportunity after a couple of long nicotine-less hours, Dazzler gets out as well. Gavin reluctantly hands him two cigarillos, tries to light one for him but the cheap lighter's flint buckles.

Guy's treated himself royally during his few hours of solitude in the shape of a local prostitute Tilly, who's sat up in his bed with her legs open. Her nickname Tilly Lick derives from Guy's specific borderline obsession with licking her out, which he's indulging in right now. A privilege he pays handsomely for, ninety pounds per half hour to be exact. While there isn't a whole lot to Tilly, naturally somewhat of a looker without taking all that much care of herself, she's the envy of rival local, more conventionally desirable prostitutes. This is on account of her practically nailed on one hundred and eighty pounds' worth of business a week guaranteed from Guy for at least two of these sessions. It's easy money, easier than shagging the bloke anyway. Dirt-cheap rent on her Maesgeirchen second floor flat allows her to get by solely on his custom most weeks.

"Give us a grumble will you! Making me think I've lost it," Guy insecurely asks, using this opportunity to pop up his head for much needed air before getting back to work.

76

Tilly snidely smirks back once he's not looking. This is Guy's one and only special request, that she dishes out the odd bit of encouragement towards what he knows deep down are his faltering abilities, despite the catalogue of practice. Tilly puts slightly more effort into the forced moaning. Fierce recurring OCD symptoms as of late shift her focus toward the state of the stale stenching room and sight of a condom used by Guy on her an entire month prior. For his forty-ninth birthday, he splurged out on a intercourse treat. Slam goes the front door, bringing an abrupt end to proceedings, Gavin being the culprit as he stands with Dazzler and Gwyn. After barely a few seconds, the doorbell starts going as well.

"Wakey wakey Gibbo lad!" Gavin shouts.

Guy bounces up and hastily throws on his vintage dark blue Levi's. "Who does this barbaric disruption of my leisure think they are?" He squares over to the window and any short-lived swagger evaporates after peeping out. "Fucking rozzers the lot!" He throws a white button-up shirt on.

Tilly shrugs, safe in the knowledge an ancient fling with Gavin will safeguard her from any trouble.

"I know I had three minutes left, but I need you to go."

"Not here for a laugh am I." Tilly expectantly holds out her hand.

"Paid for a five-session bulk deal last Friday!" Guy insists. His memory of the double session he summoned her over for on Sunday eludes him following that night's heavy session on the Xanax with Pedr.

"Well if that's how you want it to go," Tilly sarcastically says as she waltzes over to the curtain and opens it. "He's got three minutes left! Have some respect will you?!" She shouts.

Guy hauls Tilly out of sight by her shoulders and hands her a hundred and twenty pounds, a thirty quid tip! Tilly deviously smirks, fantasising about the top draw gram bag of flake that'll be flying up her hooter while Britain's Got Talent's on.

"Just make sure you fuck off out the back," Guy hesitantly insists.

Tilly shrugs, slowly counts the money on the way out, and bows down to Guy sarcastically. "A truly staggering performance squire," she says in a posh voice.

Guy dashes into the bathroom and swirls green Listerine mouthwash around his gob, mainly out of fear, fear of being taunted again for his vaginal-smelling breath many look out for given his local sexual reputation. He slicks his receding thin hair to the side with thick red Dax wax and, hurried by the constantly chirping doorbell, rushes to the door. By the front door lies the shattered bottle of vodka sprinkled in the corridor. He sweeps it up with a dustpan and brush which Gavin sneakily peeks through the letterbox and catches. When he eventually opens the door, the sight of Dazzler standing with police supersedes the arousing anxiety of his own wrongdoing. He glares daggers at Dazzler.

"Wouldn't be happening if you gave me enough for train." Dazzler barges past and scuttles into the house. Guy clenches his fist and throws an imaginary punch Dazzler's way as he passes.

"Your lad's been a massive help. Co-operated fully!" Gavin sadistically says.

"Bugle kind of morning then?" Gwyn asks while wiping his nostril.

"What's he told you about bugle?" Guy says with his eyes well and truly flared up.

Gwyn and Gavin look at each other with a wry smile. "Well, we keep getting calls about your barmy little seshes," Gavin tenderly claims.

"Which we're absolutely torn up about not being invited to, may I add," Gwyn gibingly adds, cutting Gavin off.

"Bugle frothing out your hooter, Tilly lick upstairs, glass shattered all over the shop.. who said we don't want a bit of that?" Gavin sarcastically asks.

Guy rolls up his sleeves and tenses his chest. "What I do in my house is my shout."

Having been all for the gradual winding up of Guy, Gwyn snaps. His inexperience comes into play here as he puffs out his chest and gets in Guy's face. Gavin wedges himself in between them.

"Wow, wow, yes, yes it is. But when you're tormenting your neighbours, shitting on your little one's well-being." Gavin says.

"Am I under arrest? Do you have a warrant?" Guy calmly asks after pulling away from the fracas and semi-composing himself.

"Not this time mate. But that pit you keep though Gibbo--" Gavin shakes his head. "Dazzler will end up in care, now we don't want that."

"Deadbeat cunt deserves it though, all the neighbours, lads down the pub, knowing he's fucked right up," Gwyn cunningly remarks.

"Ffocin' tâw gont!" Gavin screams.

Guy's briefly-found composure evaporates, and he squares back up to Gwyn. Gavin applies all his might and size advantage to pry them apart. Guy throws a left then right hook combination at Gwyn that he bobs his head clear of, with the power having been deflected by Gavin's strong hand in his chest. Gavin judo flips Guy over his back, sending him crashing into the squalid garden's turf, flat on his back.

Gavin whips out his police baton. "Don't start Gibbo. My night shift at cells tonight."

Working alone overnight offers a free pop at handing Guy the right jail cell hiding he's dreamed of serving him without repercussions – as per the local police force's unofficial stance on those who assault their officers. Guy wriggles backwards on the floor and stands up by the doorway, dusting his grass-stained top down as Gavin and Gwyn head back to their car.

Gwyn pokes his head out of the window as Gavin roughly starts the engine. "Have a fucking cracker with the hep c our mate!" He shouts out, his face rasping red and sweaty. Guy swaggers over and hurls a small rock on the car roof as it pulls off.

Dazzler's slouched forward on the living room sofa, an L-build readily prepared from thick red rizlas awaits as he sprinkles chopped up ashtray remnants into it. Stig flying around the Top Gear track plays off their outdated widescreen telly with a chunky back. Guy bursts in, nearly knocking the door clean off its hinges and squares up to Dazzler.

"Co-operated did you ey?" Guy bats Dazzler's joint off the table.

"Did I fuck!" Dazzler says, deeply offended to have been accused of such a thing.

"I've never been so ashamed!"

"They gave me a lift you smack rat."

Guy yanks Dazzler up by the neck and pins him against the wall. "Nerve on you, talking to me like that! After you brought the fucking rozzers here, telling them I don't give you any dough."

"It was either a lift here or A&E. And how would that have gone for you?" Dazzler wipes the accidental spit pellets pelted into his face during Guys outburst.

Guy's jaw drops, the shame he'd endure should his son be taken into care flutters before his eyes. All the bullshit he'd have to make up, oh, and if Cody, his wholesale speed dealer were to find out, his prices on half ounces would skyrocket. While knowing he's in the wrong and been done a solid favour by Dazzler, he daren't show it. He lets go of the boy.

"Full of fucking shit aren't you, full of shit." Guy chucks on his light blue, shrunk in the wash Derfel denim jacket. "And for what? Your mother would be proud, proud of the little slime ball that's coming of you. Ungrateful little sods, the both of you." He mumbles while gathering his phone, keys and dodgy duty-free Bulgarian tobacco. "You see what your life would have been like without me. Disgrace, the pair of you, ungrateful fucking sods." He slams the door behind him, rattling the door frame.

Dazzler scoops up what remains of his joint off the floor, seemingly unaffected by what is a semi-standard occurrence on his deranged father's comedowns.

Chapter 6 - Double drop

Perched on a high street bench, Frankie miserably chats on the phone to Universal Credit after an aimless afternoon of pottering around town. A skinny spliff dangles in between his fingers, one saved for hours with it being his last joint. Pissed-up fresher students stumble around, loudly berating the lack of pubs in comparison to their respective hometowns. A crowd of rowdy Bangor 1876 fans chant 'Oh Bangor aye oh aye' out the front of Skerries, their go-to pre-match boozer as they tank themselves up for a Friday evening clash under the floodlights against arch rivals Rhyl. An elderly busker rocking yellow tinted glasses and an all-black outfit hammers out guitar riffs and ripples out doom style poems with his deep voice. A pile of high value coins lie in front of him in a cotton pouch, consistently being added to by pedestrians.

"But as it should say on the *records*, I let Colin know, and that miserable fuck at McDonald's," Frankie assertively says, trying everything in his power to remain calm.

"The system stipulates that you fulfill your work search commitments, which in this case was to work the nighttime McDonald's shifts, we simply have no record of this dubious claim of yours," Karl the job centre assistant sternly asserts.

"My brother could be in danger at night! How many times?"

"I have no doubt that could be deemed a fairly valid reason," Karl clinically adds, losing patience with Frankie and interrupting him.

"Yeah, yeah, it is a valid reason isn't it. I agree. So why am I belting it out, again, and a fucking 'gain?"

"I won't tolerate aggression such as this, there's nowhere else to turn, so you have to put up with us I'm afraid."

"All right. Just don't wanna' starve to death. Lot on the line here."

Byron Wee wee prowls down the street accompanied by Damien Hayward, his old cell mate from HMP Berwyn, or Damo as he prefers to be known. He has every bit the cunning, mysterious edge slapped on him you'd expect from someone convicted of filming two fifteen-year-old girls performing sex acts on one another. An act of deviance he served only ten months inside for, in part down to his wealthy parents. With both being early investors in cryptocurrencies, they hired him a top draw barrister as their last charitable deed before disowning him entirely. Bright brown Doc Martins and a smart padded brown suede jacket on his back sticks out drastically compared to Byron's worn out, unfashionable blue and white striped track jacket and trouser combination. Their connection is mainly fuelled by mutual sadism and both having been loners on the inside. Byron on account of his tendency to bail on paying drug debts and brazenly bragging about his *'free haul'*, while Damo revolted even the most hardened of criminals at HMP Berwyn due to the seedy nature of his crimes. Fearing his tarnished local reputation would make Wrexham a sketchy place to be following his release, Damo decided to give his period on license a go in Bangor. Partly out of hope that despite the damning daily post article detailing his crime, he'd be afforded some level of anonymity in the new area, which his flashy outfit won't help him achieve. Byron spots Frankie and outstretches his arm to halt Damo, who's distracted by a group of loud, dolled-up university students marching their way into Peep nightclub.

"Ninety-one fucking days. You're not just grabbing food out of my mouth are you though," Frankie desperately pleads having calmed down minimally.

"I wish there was anything I could do to help you Frankie," Karl lethargically says.

"Now this is the issue we're having; you're choosing not to! You are fucking there to help."

"At the end of the day, we're following a system, doing what we're told mate."

"Just doing what you're told! It don't mean you're not going down with them one day, those privileged, out of touch fascist ring stings telling you what's what. When world order's gone to shit, and there's mayhem left right and centre, they won't forget about you cunts, on the phones, doing what you're told. You'll get it as well you know. And I'll be right fucking there, howling at the lot of you. Piteous rotter of a bloke."

Still observing from a safe distance, Byron enthusiastically pitches his plans for Frankie to Damo. "They own the gaff mate, proper attic, and, Gibbo rigs the 'leccy," He boisterously claims.

"Decent is it?" Damo deviously nods, encouraged by this potential development.

"Fucking right. And not only that, pair of them get through bucket loads of gear."

"What are your K and green levels like though?" Damo reluctantly asks, never being one to share his stash.

"Enough."

"I ain't dishing out tasters this time if he makes fattys."

An internal promise made after the last docile adolescent cuckooing victim of theirs made half gram joints all night. During the customary two-day grooming period of getting them on side, it's a tried and tested tactic to dish them out drugs non stop.

"Won't be an issue laa', few bongs each, odd spliff here and there, few bumps of K, get him all beholden on us." Byron reassuringly says.

Damo grins and nods, with the manipulative side to the game of cuckooing being something he relishes, something his natural sadistic core thrives off. With the dishing out drugs duty delegated, he's ready for action.

"Left wing my arse, next time you slag off Borris, or Nigel Farage, take a decent look at yourself, because you're living in the fucking spirit of their societal image," Frankie tells Karl. "Rat!" He shouts down the mic and lobs the phone at a wall to end the call.

A well-spoken Bangor University professor in marine biology named Hugh, stood at least ten metres away from the phones flight, approaches Frankie. "And what would you have done if that had hit someone?" He snidely asks in a posh Kent accent.

Frankie glares upwards his way. Before having the chance to respond, Damo and Byron dash over and Damo gets in Hugh's face.

"How do you want your day to go?" Damo chillingly asks.

Hugh cowers and turns around to run away, Damo shoves him in the back and boots him in the heel, sending hapless old Hugh's balance into disarray. He scurries off with a minor limp. Frankie's gawps in stunned silence, a part of him feeling grateful, having never had anyone stick up for him in such a way. Guy commonly allowed tons of grief hurled Frankie's way pass in the subconscious hope it'd condition him to accept abuse from him.

Byron picks up Frankie's cracked phone and buoyantly presents it to him. "Nothing a bit of lovin' won't sort."

A mildly cracked screen, a chip on the volume up button and the power still working is a result Frankie's content with. Not that a new screen's on the cards with his newfound dire financial predicament.

"Pleasure to meet you man. Damo." Damo holds his hand out with an eerie smile on him oozing creepiness and inauthenticity.

Not clear enough for Frankie however, as it pierces through his impressionable guard, despite a lingering suspicion that this could be the Damo buying his twelve-year-old brother beers.

"Frank," Frankie flatly says, cautiously shaking Damos hand with transient vigour.

Damo and Byron take a seat either side of Frankie simultaneously. "That wild look in your eyes, tells me you could do with getting fucking spangled lad," Byron playfully proposes.

"Nah, can't mate. Sanctioned I am," Frankie drearily responds.

"Sack lunch col, up to his dirty old tricks," Byron sympathetically mutters.

"Good and proper." Frankie resentfully holds up the remnants of his mostly smoked joint. "Last joint the lot." He takes a last look at it before flicking it into a bush.

Damo turns away and rolls his eyes, agonized by the mere thought of both sharing some of the first half ounce bag of weed bought in a year, failing miserably to grasp the bigger picture of lucrative profits should this mission succeed. "Wee wee's got a load of green, ain't you mate?" Damo turns around, full of smiles once again.

"Yeah fuck money, weed, it's all sorted! Let's get you out of this grot hole and back to ours for a few jars." Byron leans over and whispers in Frankie's ear. "Bit of Kenny going if you want to get a bit of a wob wob wobble on."

Calling the stuff *Kenny* is a stretch with it being more of a research grade drug resembling vague aspects of ketamine.

Frankie grins, itching to relive the sensation of k holing, an experience first endured at the age of fifteen after nicking a few lines worth from Pedr's bag as he slept off a forty-eight-hour session at the family house.

"Ninety-one days of no dole meetings, if you look at the bright side of it," Damo chimes in.

Frankie ponders internally. Not at the invite to get wrecked, that's something he needs no second thoughts about. His dilemma lies more with the guilt of leaving

Dazzler home alone at the mercy of Guy and his cretin entourage while they party hard. However, with Guy being mostly a creature of habit, Frankie doubts the likelihood of him hosting two weeknights on the bounce and eventually nods. Byron and Damo wildly cheer.

"Sweet as." Byron cracks open three small bottles of Foster's Radler using the wall ledge and passes them out. He takes an almighty chug of his, not enjoying it one bit. "Foster's fucking Radler?"

Damo shrugs and smirks back wickedly. A two-percent beverage won't even scratch Byron's sides having survived purely on a few cans of the three times stronger Carlsberg special brew a night since his release. Byron shakes up an unopened bottle, cracks it on the wall and sprays it around like a winning formula one driver. It mostly lands on the busker, showering his sleeping bag and only set of clean clothing in sticky lemon lager. Undeterred, the busker carries on playing, albeit in a more sinister tone. A police siren whirls briefly in the distance and the boys power walk up a steep, grubby thin path barely visible to the naked eye, littered in substandard patchy graffiti and used nos canisters.

With all out of breath at the top, especially Byron, they take a little breather before another steep incline on route back to Byron and Damo's halfway house building. Having chugged his Foster's Radler while cantering up the hill,

Damo pings the bottle powerfully towards an open green wheelie bin in the distance. Only it misses wildly, flies right through a terraced house's open window and shatters in their living room.

"OI!" Llŷr Mental the house's owner bellows out. This time the boys do leg it. Had Llŷr the energy left to catch them after smoking a quarter ounce of weed that day, they'd have been in right trouble. Self-proclaimed as the 'hardest lad in Bangor', he's more than capable of battering the three of them all by himself.

They approach the dull, run-down-looking halfway house. Part of its surrounding dry stone wall crumbled into the pavement and onto the edge of the road weeks prior, pathetically shielded by a few orange road fences. In the courtyard, a group of lads gather around for the customary Wednesday night halfway house piss up drinking either Jack Daniels or vodka. Bringing his usual alpha male and ADHD energy, Derfel Huws energetically raps Welsh grime lyrics. In part, to channel the trauma stemming from their lack of boom box, after an irritated neighbour smashed it with a baseball bat following three consecutive nights of outdoor residential progressive Techno raves. While he doesn't live at the hostel, his institutionalization means the place makes him feel at home. Having spent the majority of his teenage and adolescent years behind bars, he tends to know three quarters of the recently released prisoners there at any given time. As such, he is deemed the place's unofficial entertainment manager and a part of the furniture. Being at home with his passive, naive wife and three young children under five is unbearable for him, responsibilities he's long deemed his late twenties aren't worth losing over.

Sully's sullenly sat in a deck chair sipping some JD honey, bought with money made by selling four old Xbox 360 games at CEX in order to drown his dole sanction sorrows. Sat next to him is *'Greasy'* Steve Barnes, a true career criminal and a generational hero to budding criminal sorts in the local area. A reputation only enhanced by having two years added onto his last prison sentence after being paid by a county lines kingpin to bite a bloke's ear off in prison. This poor old sap left a love bite on the dealer's wife's ear of all places, and this was deemed sufficient revenge. What made it all the more barbaric was that Steve had one month left until release and did the deed for nothing more than a marginally improved cell, stronger TV signal on that side of the prison and a window wider by a couple of inches being the only upgrades.

On BBQ duties, flamboyantly grilling streaky bacon and flipping it around needlessly multiple times, is the energetic, lanky Ali Box. A well-meaning lad in comparison to the creeps keeping his company, and a Maes G boy through and through who loves a secret acid techno rave in abandoned Llanberis quarries. After leading a relatively crime-free life until sinking into cocaine addiction, he served three and half years in prison having been copped with five hundred MDMA pills at Gottwood festival.

"I'll get a speaker me. Don't care where it's from. Give us a decent line yeah, bit of a slug, and I'm fucking telling you now, I'll be out there flying until I get one. Diet's fucked if I don't," Derfel frantically belts out while nobody truly listens.

"It's absolutely brama here lad," Byron giddily tells Frankie as they strut through the original Victorian style preserved gate and into the courtyard. "Su mai wai!" He chants with his thumb up sideways. All ignore him other than Ali.

"Wee wee lad, how were your fifteen minutes for seventy bar?" Ali jeeringly asks.

"Fifty it was you prick!" Byron angrily picks up one of the value white hot dog buns next to the BBQ.

"It's all right aye, got plenty of action behind bars didn't you lad," Ali sneers.

"More than you'd ever know." Byron demandingly holds out his bun as Ali theatrically tips in a single rasher of bacon. A part of it's close to falling out but is saved by Ali's sharp reflex reactions. Without hesitation, Byron bites deep into the bap and nods approvingly. "Level one BTEC hall of fame if you carry on at this level."

"Didn't want to say so myself." Ali holds a bacon bap in each hand for Frankie and Damo.

Frankie nervously accepts and once in his hands, he ferociously bites into it, grateful for the chance to rid himself of the hunger pains plaguing him since wolfing down a BBQ rib rustlers burger the previous night.

"Vegan mate," Damo snarls after leaving Ali holding the sandwich for an awkward amount of time.

Ali hollowly stares at Damo before lowering his bottom lip in disgust and turning away. Not only is he sensitive to rejection, but he's also deeply threatened by the slim possibility that vegan food could take over – leaving his days of eating real meat numbered. This projects itself in a hatred for anything or anyone vegan. Having finished their baps and gained no inkling that their presence is welcome, Frankie, Damo, and Byron head towards the building's front door. Derfel suddenly appears and blocks their entrance.

"With this being a fine five-star establishment of the highest order, I can't be allowing you through without adhering to our strict but fair Covid testing rules." Derfel puts on a rough formal accent and points at Damo and Byron. "Now, you two almost definitely have aids, and science has proven it kills Covid off so, you're both exempt. But you sir, not so lucky I'm afraid."

Derfel sternly passes Frankie a cotton bud and a plastic vile. He nervously sticks it up each nostril for a few seconds, twisting it when up there. His hand lightly trembles while placing them in the plastic vile as he passes them over. Derfel sticks them on the small white Covid tester kit.

"No doubt Greasy Steve will have a bit of something nice back if you've given him Covid," Ali sniggers, most chuckle at his remark.

"Be nothing fucking nice about it. Can see how tight he is from here," Greasy Steve chillingly remarks.

Derfel gazes up at Frankie apprehensively as the test comes up as positive, a chorus of 'ohhh' crescendos from Sully and Ali, building up the tension.

"Shit, I'll just go you know," Frankie mumbles before briskly shooting off.

After a few seconds everyone bursts out laughing, with Damo and Byron joining in slightly after the rest. Frankie gazes back and, after being slow to realize he's been stitched up, trudges back over and heads into the building with Byron and Damo.

"Double drop boys, learnt this one in pen," Ali boasts.

With a spatula in each hand and two bits of bacon on each, he simultaneously flips them over flamboyantly onto two baps. After misjudging his power, the bap closest to Steve splats on the floor, with Steve only narrowly avoiding the greasy bacon landing on his brand new light brown Timberland steel toe caps. Furious at the near miss, he leaps up in a fit of rage.

"Double fucking drop. What are you doing?" Steve shouts.

"Oh here we go, battered a few spastics in Berwyn, now he thinks he's fucking hardest cunt in Maes G," Ali boldly responds to the far bulkier Steve.

"Calm down grease lad, Al'll do you another one," Derfel says.

"Last of the bastard bacon in it. Gives it all to them weirdo crusties before he feeds his own mates! Go on, piss off to fucking Spar now," Steve demands. All the while, Ali squirts an excessive amount of mustard into a bun. "Get your strapnel out lad, before I fucking snap you, get us a few special brews and all while you're at it."

Ali lobs the mustard covered bun into Steve's face, landing most of the stuff in his eyes and temporarily blinding him. With Steve bent down trying to clear his eyesight, Ali takes the opportunity and lands a sweeping head kick on him owing to a brief dalliance in muay thai in preparation for his prison sentence. Despite his obscured vision, Steve lands a right hook clean on Ali's jaw, but Ali stands firm and a brutal brawl ensues. As they trade hammer blows, offering little head movement to avoid the others' punches, Derfel eventually gets in the middle and throws them both aside by their collars. In the midst of the chaos, Sully calmly sneaks back inside.

Byron presents his damp, dirty self-contained studio room with a thin window placed high up on the wall barely letting sunlight in. An A1 sized poster of the band Dope dangles on the wall with its top right hand corner detached. Deliberate-looking punch holes occupy the white wall's cracked, uneven plaster as well as black damp mould patches. A crusty pile of dry, used tea bags take up the corner of the stain ridden kitchen surface. Fruit flies happily hover and breed among the tea bag mound and sugar caked into the surface. Frankie and Damo wince at the unpleasantly stale stench, Damo covers his nose with the top of his jumper.

"DMT bender with the lads or what?" Damo barely audibly muffles, he sweeps a pile of crumbs off Byron's duvet and takes a seat on the bed.

"Spangled isn't the word laa'. Just me it was aye," Byron enthusiastically says.

"All right then man," Damo lethargically responds, already sorry for asking.

"Conked out in that corner there. But in my head, I were in Dickie's boat yard aye, chilling on the pebs, after a tidy spring evening hammering nos up Bangor Mountain, smashing down the most brama Shahin's double special burger, while at the same time.." Byron loses momentum towards the end, his crack cravings affecting the fluidity of his speech. Damo rolls his eyes and tucks his smoke. Byron regains his composure. "While at the same time, getting a fucking tit wank off an horrible, scabby, four out of ten at best Maes G mermaid mate."

Damo and Frankie gaze at each other and howl in disbelief derived laughter.

"Four out of ten yeah?" Damo asks.

"That's with whatever fucking 1080p goggles DMT puts on you that is. Minging, I'm telling you!" Byron shudders.

"Off your head on a bit of classic spice again," Damo says before once again bursting out laughing. "Maes G mermaid man!"

"On my little boy's life," Byron defiantly claims.

After a few unsatisfactory spliffs and bumps of ketamine, time simply stands still for Byron, who just can't get into the swing of things. By 5PM, he's had enough and bails on his self-imposed 8PM deadline for a pipe of crack. Having done so for five days straight in an effort to curb the amount of profits he smokes, an unrestrained evening of debauchery is in order. With his head stuck out of the window blatantly visible from the street, he lights his oval bowled glass pipe and takes a hefty hit double the size of his usual. He used to smoke it out in the communal yard, preferring the fresh air. However, having one of the many halfway house addicts spotting him out there, pestering to swap a couple of quids worth for a pinch of dirty, duty-free tobacco had become the bane of his life. Damo racks up four lines of ketamine, unconvincingly pretending to listen to Frankie, who's already tipsy after two Foster's Radler due to his near empty stomach.

"Don't get haze like this much now do you no?" Frankie says, his voice affected by the harshness of Byron's half gram spliff of purple haze that he tokes on.

"More of a south east skunk fella me," Damo coldly claims. He smoothly snorts the heftiest of the four lines with a rolled-up orange train ticket and twitches after.

"Only got the Hirael hippies shotting that round here," Frankie says.

Information Frankie should not be passing on to such menaces. Brothers Jed and Herbie Barnivelt, commonly referred to as 'Jed and Herbie Hippy', have historically been targeted by Byron and his callous acquaintances. Between five and ten thousand pounds worth of weed has been burgled from their house on four separate occasions, with the subsequent paranoia forcing them to move between four of the county's villages in the last two years. One of these events in the last few months culminated in their beloved dog Seb being stabbed to death as he attacked intruders who were after their gear.

"Got to watch it with weirdos like that." Damo scrapes a third off the top of two of the lines to make a chunkier one at the end and snorts it.

"Dirty bastards them. Yeah, they've got banging smoke, out of this fucking world in fact, but what percentage of them dirty fingernails have touched my buds? You know, not only will some of that filth be making up the weight of my ten bag aye, but they're also literally putting shit down my lungs," Frankie says, a two-faced statement given his strong working relationship with the pair.

With no interest in what Frankie's saying, Damo cuts him off by passing him the tray of lines. "For you sir."

Frankie shrugs and takes it. "Love a little encounter with our mate Kenny."

Only half of the line shoots up Frankie's hooter before he hastily places the case on the bottom half of his leg, allowing the loose drugs on the tray to wobble dangerously.

"Careful mate!" Damo anxiously snatches the tray off Frankie. Spotting the half-finished line, he scoffs, deciding there and then that this soft fool is ripe for the picking.

Frankie leans his back on the wall, already feeling highly wavy, with his senses well and truly distorted. He slowly nods to the trap beat playing roughly off Byron's old-school Motorola. "Nice one for that," He mumbles.

Damo subtly smirks. "Mate of Wee wee's is a mate of mine."

Frankie nods. With his eyes squinted together beyond recognition, he holds out a clenched fist and fist bumps Damo. Damo turns away and cringes out of Frankie's view, repulsed by being forced to be friendly with someone he'd have no problem robbing.

After half an hour of dissociative chatter full of broken sentences, Byron decides Frankie needs waking up and throws down a packet of lemon flavoured rip rolling skins. "Bit of graft will sort you out," he says.

Frankie tears off a ten centimetre strip.

"Give them here," Byron insists. Frankie throws the packet up, and Byron tears off a foot long rip and throws that down. "Pass him the dust will you Damo."

Having just sniffed two slug sized lines of ketamine, Damo groans and, in his moderate incapacitation, manages to grab and pass a wooden tray with loose bits of small bud, crumbs, and leaf over to Frankie, who appears daunted by the task.

"All of it?" Frankie sheepishly asks.

"What do you think?" Byron restlessly fires back, frustrated at the lack of impact from his hit of crack.

Frankie lies on his chest and gets to work. Presuming he has to use what will be a hefty chunk of his own limited tobacco supply for this mammoth spliff, he reluctantly doesn't question it. Tucking the edges proves problematic for him after taking twenty minutes to get to that stage. Damo gets up and dances erratically behind him in short bursts to the rhythm of the trap beat. He picks up a pool cue, takes a few fake shots and theatrically spins it around his head. With

Frankie unsighted, Damo pretends to stick the cue up Frankie's arse from a short distance away, much to the subtle amusement of Byron. With the spliff painstakingly rolled, Frankie lights it with a jet lighter and chokes hard on the first toke.

"I'll be sound boys," Frankie splutters as snot droops out of his nose after a heavy cough.

Damo snatches the joint as Frankie runs over to the sink and buries his head in it, gagging ferociously. After getting a whiff of the stale cooking fat and dry piss covering the sink, he lifts his head out. Damo and Byron cackle at this unfolding. With the central locking door left wedged open due to a groove in the wooden lino, Sully bursts in and lobs a bag of bashed up cocaine at Byron's head. Frankie backs into the far corner and cowers fearfully out of sight.

"Gave me flat out fucking laxative shite you miserable little prick!" Sully shouts.

A school boy error on Byron's part. When packing bags of cocaine, he divides them into two categories, one stronger lot and one set of bags made deliberately weaker for those he doesn't fear. Sion Bâch, a far scrawnier lad, had been given Sully's stronger bag.

"Top draw that is, and you know it," Byron unconvincingly responds while rooted to his spot.

Sully slams Byron into the wall by his throat and holds him there. "Can't fool a cunt with chronic IBS."

With his free hand, Sully opens a nearby draw and grabs out one hundred and forty pounds. Knowing it'd be kept somewhere blatant given Byron's historical lack of subtlety with his stash spots, Sully counts it before waving the wad in Byron's face.

"That'll do for now." Sully stuffs the cash gratefully into his navy Adidas tracksuit bottoms pockets.

Damo sneaks up behind Sully, but his heavy anxious breathing gives Sully just enough time to move his head away from the swinging pool cue.

Sully throws a chopping kick upwards into Damo's liver, sending him crashing to the ground. "You can fuck off and all you nonce." He snatches the pool cue. "I'll have a bit of that."

Sully walks away examining the Powerglide cue and thinking of all the league players likely to bung him up to a bullseye for it. He turns back and aims a kick at the still floored Damo's head that deliberately doesn't connect, Damo shrieks and collapses further into the corner with his hands up. Flashbacks of the first month of rough prison treatment he received come flooding back, having copped three such beatings in this time. Something Sully observed fondly on each and every occasion.

"Just you wait," Sully coldly warns, pointing the cue at Frankie. "Stay right there and you're brama." As he walks out the door, he sticks the lock on the latch and closes it tightly, smashing it back open with a kick from the outside and bending the lock. He re-enters and tests the lock, which now doesn't work. "You're both marked. I'll be back for the rest of that, whenever I want, in whatever form it comes, day or fucking night."

Sully slams the door behind him, which bounces back open. Damo gets up, dusts off the various crumbs on his clothing from Byron's filthy floor and lobs a lighter at the door that pops, well after Sully would have realized.

With their immediate safety and privacy in doubt, the boys opt to get up and head down to the social club's pound-a-pint two hours earlier than anticipated. They head out the back and take the scenic route over Bangor Mountain, far more awkward for the short trip to the pub but neither Byron nor Damo can face Sully and his group. No doubt boasting has already taken place to anyone that will listen regarding the details of his swift and clinical triumph over the pair. Damo ushers Byron and Frankie into an outside public toilet, gets his key out then conveniently is unable to find his little pub bag of ketamine in his keg pocket. Byron reluctantly dishes them both out a couple of chunky keys worth.

Posters sporting 2000s era Microsoft art stating 'Mid-week bar a jar! Foster's, Strongbow, and Worthington's' a foot apart litter the windy corridor wall leading up to the social club. Outside in the beer garden, all five wooden benches are joined together. Forty young punk rockers scatter, most smoking weed and sniffing coke with all the paraphernalia on show. All taking full advantage of this pub's sympathy for the pound a pint goer's average customer demographic; those only content if able to adhere to their addictions. Two skaters with red flat caps on backwards land nose grinds off the edge of a bench seat one after the other, met by wild cheers.

A row of grizzly, miserable older 'day time drinkers' on stools obstruct a collectively frustrated twenty-person cue. All determined to make it as hard for those glory hunters to get served as possible, who are only at their otherwise peaceful drinking hole for pound-a-pint. One such individual not putting up with this attempted corruption of his pound a pint enjoyment is Mac: a wily punk rocker. One of the alpha males and leaders of the crew due to his fearless stunt man attitude, evidenced by his plethora of stunt and skateboarding inflicted chipped teeth. Using his rugged, thick wax rich Mohawk, he rams first through the old farts by the bar and then the crowd cueing for drinks, majestically not spilling any of the nine pints held on the tray. Most back away, no questions asked. Mac heads over to the freshly damp stained pool table, with forty pounds in notes dangling on the side, awaiting the winner of the next frame. A group of six similarly styled punks huddle around watching the game intently. As they spot Mac, they swamp him for the pints and scuttle back off to watch the game. Julian, more of a passive emo than the rest, and seven pints of cider down, chips the cue ball Mac's way. It shatters one of the pints on the tray. Mac ferociously throws the cue ball back on the table, sending multiple yellow and red balls flying.

Guy, Stacey, Sally, Razza and Pedr sit on the far end of a high stool table. Guy rubs his hands together and restlessly gazes around the pub, phased out of the ongoing, quickly-paced, erratic cocaine-fuelled conversations taking place. Not for the first time, this cliquey group are somewhat tolerating more than celebrating his presence. Itched by the nearly twelve-hour drought since he ran out of cocaine, Guy dials Byron's number.

"How are you laa'?" Byron's voicemail says.

Guy breaths a deep sigh of relief. "Wee wee mate, you're taking the fucking piss here, we all need topping up, pronto."

"If you're after our gardening work summer special, please leave a message stating the quantity of your occupational needs, after the tone," Byron's voicemail continues after a pause.

"Voicemail me you trampy little dick!" Guy shouts, trying desperately to keep a lid on the noise level.

Guy furiously re-dials, but his phone battery dies, leading him to hastily slam his Samsung on the table. Stacey glances over, weary of his outbursts and energy sapping ways but quickly continues chatting.

106

"Do us a bump or two 'till he gets here will you?" Guy asks Razza intensely, knowing he stands no chance with the others. After Razza doesn't respond, Guy taps his shoulder repeatedly. "Oi!"

Razza turns back, cutting Stacey's long-awaited chance to unload all the Ysbyty Gwynedd gossip, where she works as a porter. "Never is just a bump when you get your grubby little claws in there."

"C'mon mate! I'll give it you back," Guy pleads.

"Nah you'll guzzle it right up."

Guy sits back with his arms crossed; his face slowly turns red as he stews internally. "Prick. Wait until you haven't got any one day, I'll remember that mate!"

Razza rolls his eyes and looks back. "Hang on in there Gibbo, won't be long 'til he's here," he patronizingly says.

"Do us a key one of you?" Guy asks the table.

Stacey, Sally and Pedr ignore him without even a brief glance, all being in the same boat of not trusting him alone with their hard-earned cocaine. Guy grunts, stroppily gets up, slams his chair into the table, picks up his pint and swaggers over to the pool table – where Mac and Julian are engaged in an enthralling game. Flying from the joy of his forty quid win, of which the winnings hang perilously on the edge of his skinny black jeans' pockets, Julian is potting balls for fun, and knocks his fifth in a row down to leave a tricky long range shot on the black.

107

"Fiver and a key's worth of bugle says I'll wipe the fucking floor with you," Guy says right in Mac's face.

"Tenner'll just about get me out of bed," Mac calmly responds.

"Sweet as!" Guy slams a tenner down on the table.

Mac does the same and looks menacingly over at Julian, who smashes the black ball in without looking.

"Rack them up then old school." Mac flings the triangle over and Guy fumbles it pathetically.

Taking the opportunity with Guy's focus laying elsewhere, Pedr stealthily gets the group's attention and they giddily sneak off towards the bathroom. Having won the lag and deciding to break, Guy makes a meal of his break off, slamming the cue ball dangerously low. After smashing the pack of colours, it pings off the table, out the open back door and into the sea of punk rockers outside. One of them uses their skateboard to bat it back in after having it bowled his way by his fourteen-year-old brother – who's out on his first proper night on the lash. Julian catches it with one hand and lays it down for Mac as he cues up his shot from above the baulk line. After some miniscule adjustments, Mac smashes his first red in, barely giving Julian a chance to move his hand. Two simple pots follow, and in full swing, he misses an inexcusable fourth shot and kicks the air.

"Already feeling a tingle down my hooter," Guy boldly claims despite having all of his balls to pot.

With Mac's break having generously spread the balls, Guy makes slim pickings of them. Most being short to mid-range bar one beautifully doubled into the middle pocket. He misses a straightforward cut on the black but with a stroke of good fortune, it zips off the cushion and nestles into the top right-hand pocket. Guy struts over and presents his key, Mac shoves a bit of cocaine on the end and Guy runs into the corner to devour it up his bad nostril. With his theory being that should he have miniscule supply, the varying degree of pain that comes from sniffing up his deviated left nostril adds a bit more bite to the sensation.

Now fuelled up for at least the next twenty minutes, Guy storms back towards Mac. "Name your price boy," he gallantly proposes.

"Glad someone's thinking big time!" Mac approvingly says.

This time Guy makes no mistake, nailing his break off shot, potting three red balls and one yellow. However, the white trickles in as well. With two shots at an open table, Mac clears up the colours with no issues, but rattles his black in the pocket's jaws, slamming the pub's cue tip on the table in response. Guy gets down for his shot but is distracted by the now empty table once occupied by Razza and co.

"Slimy little dicks!" Guy shouts.

Betrayed by their minor abandonment, Guy chucks the cue aside and storms off to the bathroom, needlessly barging through the door. In turn, startling a feminine looking emo meticulously waxing his goth style hair in the mirror. Guy dips his finger in the blue Dax hair wax pot, puts it in his mouth and violently spits it out into the sink, narrowly avoiding the emo with his spit. After sticking his ear on all five closed toilet cubicles, Guy clocks subdued collective giggling from one on the far end and hammers on the door.

"Fuck sake," Stacey mutters.

"Saved any for me or what?" Guy desperately grovels.

They let him into the dingy cubicle. Stacey rolls her eyes and reluctantly hands Guy the nearly empty bag sporting a measly few crumbs. Despite this, his grateful eyes light up as he scrambles to shovel a key out of his pocket. Everyone swiftly squeezes past and shuffles out of the cubicle without Guy as much as blinking an eyelid, leaving the door wide open. Guy ferociously rips open the bag, dabs his finger around the corners and rubs it on his gum.

Eventually, Guy stumbles back up to the pool table, pumped and ready to win enough to pay for his night's drinks. Julian and Mac race each other side by side to chug their pints of Worthington's. A tray of four full and four empty pint glasses lies next to them. Guy barges past, knocking into Mac and causing a splutter in his chug, but without stopping him from beating Julian. Guy stiffly gets down for a shot with steely determination, not realizing an entire new frame has been set up.

"You chose the powder route in life old school, game's up," Julian defiantly tells Guy.

"Well I'll have my dough back off you then squire," Guy sternly demands.

Julian scoffs and shakes his head. "Fifteen-minute rule! You pissed off, and your game's up, along with anything else that comes with it."

As Julian gets down for a shot, Guy knees him the ribs. Mac barges Guy up against the wall with his forearm and Julian quickly recovers, cornering Guy with Mac. Guy throws and misses a few wild punches that are easily evaded, leaving his midriff open for Julian to smash a bar stool into. This rocks but doesn't floor him as it's partly blocked. Razza pulls Mac and Julian away by their neck from behind with one hand each and drops them on the floor.

"Enough!" Razza demands with a grizzly glare.

Mac and Julian smirk victoriously, shrug and strut back over to their tray of pints. "Tah for the jars Gibbo." Mac sarcastically holds up a glass.

Guy charges at Mac but is easily held back by Razza. "Get over there until Wee wee gets here," Razza urges, which Guy duly does in an almighty strop.

It's Guy's lucky day, he doesn't have to wait long. Out from the wilderness of the sketchy main road public toilet, having finally consumed their desired share of ketamine, Damo and Byron appear in the smoking area with Frankie lingering just behind.

Among the ten smokers out the front, no one is as cheery to see Byron as Richie Lloyd, a true Llanerchymedd lad who's Bangor rugby club's long-serving first choice tight head prop. Down to his local fame among rugby supporters, he's a well-known and consistent presence in the pub scene. Having managed to shun drugs for most of his adult life, preferring any kind of cheap cider, he's recently fallen deep into the trap of craving cocaine when he drinks. Tempted into it over time by one of the vast array of dealers who swamp out both of his favourite drinking holes. He approaches Byron and tightly squeezes him in a hug, his towering frame doing well not to snap his ribs.

"Su mai wa?" Byron breathlessly asks after being released by Richie.

"Ey spot on de. All about that jet fuel of yours de boi," Richie joyfully declares. Having only been into cocaine for the last four months, his low tolerance ensures that even Byron's substandard drivel works like jet fuel for him.

Richie's nervous bald-headed mate Terry Clogs anxiously giggles with a beady smile, struggling to maintain eye contact with anyone. This demonstrates the exact lack of confidence that's caused five years on the books of Bangor rugby club to yield him only a handful of brief substitute appearances, when they're at least fifty points up. Guy gleefully spots Byron through the window and frantically takes fifty pounds off Razza and a hundred off Pedr – who, as usual, is paying for Stacey's on the false premise of getting it back on payday.

"Plate in the microwave like I showed you?" Byron asks Richie.

"Fucking right lad. Don't mind doing us one on tick 'till next bar a jar no?" Richie says.

Before Byron gets a chance to respond, Guy comes crashing through the door and stands in-between Byron and Richie. "Good to see you my mate!" He cheerfully declares.

"Yeah." Byron tries to shuffle past Guy.

"Do us the usual Wee wee boy," Guy insists.

"Yeah, yeah, fucking move for a sec first mate," Byron restlessly tells him.

"Eighth in four separate bags, in case you've forgotten." Guy brazenly waves three hundred pounds in notes around.

Byron forcefully shoves Guy's pre-wrapped order into his chest and snatches the money while anxiously looking left and right. He's not helped by the added paranoia of his dwindling crack hit, and the subsequent ketamine devoured before arriving. Although it's widely known this rugged establishment turns somewhat of a blind eye, they see a lack of subtly that could get the place in trouble as impertinent, and will ban him should they catch it on CCTV.

113

That will hurt Byron's income dramatically, given the guaranteed business that comes with the extra level of intoxication arising from cheap pound pints. With that promising start to what Byron hopes will be a highly profitable night, he assuredly leads the boys inside. Freshly wobbly having gone in hard with their pre-pub ketamine bumps, with Frankie particularly disorientated, they slowly head in through the grade two listed building's original front door and down the windy corridor. But not before taking in some of the original unnerving, dark celtic art on a poster before eventually reaching the pub area. Frankie's taken aback by the swathes of drunken mayhem and disruptively bright lights, the ketamine high overwhelming him in these chaotic surroundings.

"Damo's got first round sorted, haven't you lad?" Byron cheerily declares.

"Oh yeah course," Damo resentfully responds, trying everything in his might not to appear so. He stands at the back of the hefty cue for a few seconds before impatiently sighing and maneuvering around its outer edges, barging others out of the way without being challenged.

"Let's get you sat down then boio, few swift jars will be just the slap around the chops you need." Byron leads Frankie to a table, spots Razza in the corner and whacks his thumb up at him. "How are ya'!"

114

Razza scowls with a forced half-smile. He notices Frankie with him and ponders, clearly worried about the identity of Frankie's company as he chugs half a pint. Byron glares at the sticky, poorly wiped table and pulls out a chair. Frankie stumbles into it and nearly falls off the side.

"Fucking hell lad, thought you were a proper ket head these days!" Byron pitifully remarks as he takes a seat opposite by the wall containing framed pictures of Puffin Island.

A brief silence beholds them as Byron and Frankie scour their surroundings, with Byron's focus glued to a group of eight loud, attractive, ordinarily dolled up women in their twenties.

Byron scowls and turns back to Frankie. "Don't even feel the urge you know, fucked ragged inside I was, need a break if anything!"

"Well, it can't be hard to come by in Berwyn after lights out," Frankie unconvincingly suggests.

"Nah Frank lad, I ain't a bender me," Byron insists.

Damo miserably approaches the table carrying nine pints of Carlsberg on a tray. He cracks out an inauthentic smile as he gets closer and puts the tray down.

"Cheers mate," Frankie says.

"You are welcome," Damo says with forced sincerity.

Byron nods his head in the direction of the women. Damo sits down slurping his pint, transfixed by what he sees, his legs dangle open suggestively while his eyes dart around decidedly in all directions.

"So how did that work then Wee wee, getting laid flat out inside, daily conjugals with the second wife, or what?" Frankie curiously asks.

"Fuck that! Nah lad, warden herself, on the reg," Byron boasts. "This drip of a screw. He'd never check my socks."

Damo gets up and assertively swaggers over to two of the group of women, best friends Glesni and Delyth. Glesni, the more confident of the two, is happy to see him. Delyth, who's on her first night out and overwhelmed by her surroundings, stands there anxiously. Byron veers off as he stares bewilderingly at Damo typing his phone number into Glesni's phone.

"Get in there Damo!" Byron cheers.

"Go on mate!" Frankie adds less intensely.

Byron ponders for a second, restlessly trying to regain his train of thought.

"Son am sanna chdi," Frankie suggests after recalling Byron's troubles with the English language upon first starting primary school, due to Welsh being his first language.

"Ahh, sanna de. So I'd rock up, warden's office, eight thirty sharp, vibrator down the sock, side of the Achilles like that, and I'd be locked in 'til lunch, whether I wanted to be or not." Byron's lower lip drops. "Bit attached she got, her first con I was. Kept me right fucking busy telling you now."

In reality his sorrow derives from being clinically rebuffed by Sue, the nymphomaniac prison warden twice his age, an experience that made his prison sentence far trickier to endure.

"She'd come find you would she? Oh hello Wee wee, can I have a shag please?" Frankie sarcastically asks, with even his gullibility struggling to fall for this one.

"Nah, nah the others'd get proper jealous, nah, nah be a text, different scandalous filth every day. Let me have a phone in there, just for that." Byron boisterously winks and chugs half of a pint. "Munter by this point though I must admit. One of them. Told me she was well into her erotica screenplays back in the day. Nearly flogged one of them, five figures! A decent chunk of change back then."

"First question of many, why didn't you just keep the vibrator in the office?" Frankie asks.

Byron slaps the table, finding the task of wriggling out of his own lie unexpectedly daunting. "It was for her material! She can't write shit that hasn't happened."

Sensing his old mate floundering under the pressure of impressing Frankie, Damo passes Frankie over another pint. "Sink that down in twenty, and I'll get you three fucking more," Damo menacingly proposes.

Frankie glares mockingly at Damo, almost insulted by the challenge and sinks the full pint in ten seconds.

Terry and Richie continue to linger outside in the smoking area. Two small keys of cocaine each and their chain-smoking desires diminish the possibility of heading inside, despite being under-dressed in t-shirts on this chilly evening. Most of the old men listen in on their erratic conversation.

"Mae'r hen foi de, wythdeg un wsos dwytha, a'r unig peth mae'n goro ddeud os mae o isho sex de 'di JULIA! Ma na ddigon yn capal yn barod amdani os dwi'm yn gal off y chdi, so tyd flaen neudi, fynu grisau na 'wan." Richie theatrically imitates his father's stern Anglesey accent. Everyone listening in giggles at Terry and Richie's hysterical laugh and excessive reaction, more than the story itself.

Fresh from his cruise down the A55 to Sheffield for Q school, Alfie pulls sharply into the car park. He parks close by to Richie and Terry, needlessly dispersing the crowd when there are bundles of parking spaces in less intrusive corners. He takes his five-foot-long cue case out the of boot and balances it on the car while applying aftershave.

"Yli cont gwirion 'ma," Terry mutters.

Alfie heads towards the smoking area with an entitled air in his stride. His pink back blazer inspired by Mark Davis's style and his over-waxed hair glows under the beam of a street light as he lights up a fag. Marlboro golds this time, a rare treat and break from rolling skinny gold leaf fags all day.

Richie and Terry burst out laughing at the comical sight of Alfie. "Why are you bringing that, to pound-a-pint?" Richie judgmentally asks.

"Ain't using that joke shop selection of rods in there," Alfie declares, as if anyone who does is a waste of space. As he brushes past, Richie snatches the cue case and runs around the car park with it, pretending to cue up. Once Alfie gets closer, Richie lobs the case over his head towards Terry.

"Daliai chief!" Richie desperately shouts.

Terry drops his pint glass, which shatters on the concrete, and catches the case. Its sheer might knocks him into the wall.

"Better pray the damage is minimal. Fat fucking ring piece. No bin man double shifts will get you anywhere near out of the financial ruin I'll bury you in," Alfie claims in a childlike fit of rage.

Terry gets up and eagerly hands Alfie the case as he stares him and Richie down.

"You small time village dicks." Alfie flicks ash from his fag onto Terry's polo shirt. "Need to better spot a local legend when you see one." He flicks his fag into Terry's face as he finishes his sentence.

Richie squares up to Alfie, while clearly scared at the same time. Despite his size, Richie's combat experience is few and far between. Alfie backs away with his fist raised, and nobody follows him as he heads down the windy corridor to the pub. He swaggers in and looks around. Disappointingly for him, only a few brief judgmental glances come his way. Deflated by this, he slumps towards the now anemic cue for drinks. Gill Rowlands, a barside-stool stalwart, who only moves from his beloved right hand corner for either a piss, or for his customary squandering of a fiver in the fruit machine, carefully sips his double scotch. After catching a glimpse of Alfie in the corner of his eye, he stares him up and down, concluding his exhibition of disdain by fixating momentarily on his blazer. Gill mockingly scoffs and turns away. Guy creeps up behind Alfie and wraps his arm tightly around the back of his neck. Alfie assertively wriggles out of it, not wanting any of Guy's grubby sweat on his newly dry-cleaned blazer.

"Bottled it on the big stage, didn't you squire?" Guy intensely says after staring at Alfie in an attempt to read his body language.

Alfie's eyes light up, he clenches a fist. "Fuck that!" he blares out. "Beat Dale the lot, total clearance to seal it!"

"Oi oi!" Guy shouts and vigorously shakes Alfie by the shoulders.

"Pro tour baby," Alfie adds.

Guy throws four pounds worth of small change onto the bar with all of it scattering, some falling off the side. He jumps up and down in wild celebration.

"Had a score on you at thirty to one boy!" Guy proudly passes Alfie a pint of Strongbow.

"Oh yeah!" Alfie slides his hand into his pocket and with a beaming grin, whips out a betting slip staking thirty pounds on the same bet. "Zing!"

Guy wraps his arm around Alfie's neck, leads him a couple of steps forward, raises his pint and whistles loudly, gaining most of the room's attention.

"After heroically joining the pro snooker ranks this evening, I present to you all, Snowdonia's snooker sensation, pound-a-pint's very own baller." Guy theatrically holds both his hands out towards Alfie. "Alfie, one visit, Fenner!" Guy blares, putting on a credible Bruce Buffer impression.

Most of the pub raucously erupts. Pedr and Razza whistle and stand up out of respect. Mac and Julian enviously look on, annoyed to have had his pool momentum interrupted, Mac smashes in a few pots with excessive power.

Alfie raises his hand around the room, trembling under the boisterous response. He power walks over to Frankie's table, hesitating as he spots Damo and Byron. "Easy Wee wee," he says, barely able to withhold his grimace. "Frankie." He gazes at Damo. "All right mate?"

"Damo," Damo flatly says, half-heartedly holding out his hand. Alfie shakes it like slippery wet mackerel and sits down to an uncomfortably eerie atmosphere among the table.

"Hit the big time now lad!" Byron says with a cheeky probing grin.

Alfie rolls his eyes as he frantically searches the inner depths of his faux leather £12.99 wallet. "Long as I keep winning," he blandly says, drastically distracted by ripping out a cocaine baggy wedged in the netting of the wallet. It's empty, with the memory of licking its crumbs to settle his nerves late last night evading him. "Sucks dick for no money." He reluctantly gets forty pounds out of his wallet and passes it to Byron under the table. "Do us a half would you Wee wee?"

"You piss it then or what?" Frankie says.

"Forty-five this is lad," Byron says with flared nostrils.

Alfie exaggeratingly tears out another fiver and exchanges it with Byron for the cocaine under the table.

"Easy day's work for you no doubt?" Frankie says.

Alfie carefully examines the half gram bag under the table for quality and quantity. "Yeah mate yeah, didn't make too much of a meal of it actually," he vacantly says, dotting his head back and forth between the bag and Frankie. He smirks, funnels out a small silver house key from his tiny inside pocket and sticks it deep inside the bag of cocaine. "Dale took a few frames off me but," Alfie snorts the key emphatically. "Made him cry so, well worth it."

Frankie bursts out laughing, Byron fiercely smiles, growing frustrated by Alfie's blatant disregard for the club's unwritten rule of being subtle with your coke.

Alfie chugs most of a pint and glares disdainfully around the room. "Coming snooker hall or what?"

"Look at all these thoroughly earnt pints," Frankie says.

Alfie snatches one of Frankie's pints and slurps most of it down. Damo grits his teeth, desperate to confront him.

"Place is slammed full of noobs." Alfie snoops his head down for another quick key of cocaine. "Trial period is effective immediately as well." He winces, the tingle from the benzocaine cut into the gear catches him off guard. He shovels on an even chunkier key's worth and snorts it with the opposite nostril. "Won't look good when your month probation comes round, sacking off your first shift to stay here chugging skippy piss."

Over at the bar, Gill glowers pitifully at Alfie. "Disgrace swagging that ugly thing on TV aye!" he says to Scott the barman.

Scott rolls his eyes. He has no time for Gill's incessant verbal scolding of everything and everyone. "You give that much of a rat's arse, go and sort him out."

"Iesgo banol, would have been cuing round the block in my day de." Gill slams his pint glass down on the bar after chugging over half of it, which startles Terry as he cautiously grips a tray of four pints. Froth drips down the edge of the glasses as he edges past, wincing as the fresh scrapes and cuts on his arm brush against the increasingly impatient punters in line.

Alfie waits, stood up by the table, anxiously tapping his foot as Frankie fist bumps Byron and Damo.

"In a bit yeah lads, banging night, have to do it again!" Frankie buoyantly says.

Damo creepily winks as him and Byron nods and smiles. Once Frankie and Alfie turn their backs, Damo shudders and wipes his hand and knuckles on the table. Guy stands up and cheers savagely as they leave, and Alfie waves half-heartedly and rushes outside.

"Champion's league won't know what hit them my boy!" Guy says.

Alfie hurries to the car and fires up the engine way before Frankie leisurely makes it over, visibly lethargic from the ketamine cramps just topped off by the swift consecutive pints of lager. Between the haze of his muddled state and rolling up an L joint to have out on Old School Ken's balcony, Frankie barely notices they're heading down the windy A5 past Bethesda. He anxiously gazes up at Alfie, whose breathing is heavy, his head placed strangely forward towards the steering wheel with flared nostrils. Frankie clocks the speedometer, which reads seventy-two miles per hour.

"Trying a new club tonight are we mate?" Frankie quietly asks.

"Just wanna' wizz about for a while, bit of a drive," Alfie quickly responds. He throws Frankie a small dried snot and cocaine caked key. "Chuck a bit of bugle on that and do us a rolly will you?"

"Look, if I'm not grafting tonight, I wouldn't mind sinking a few more down bar a jar be honest with you." Frankie rolls his eyes and hands Alfie the skinny cigarette he's halfway through making. "Can you take us back?"

Alfie scoffs and throws the fag out of the window. "You ain't got a fucking job boy!" Alfie says after an eerie pause, taking his eyes off the road while he pours cocaine onto the gap between the bottom of his index finger and thumb and snorts it.

"What was all that one-month probation shite then?" Frankie sinks drearily into his seat and turns away with a scrunched up, bitter face.

"I didn't win at Q school." Alfie looks down miserably. "I ain't a pro." A tear trickles down his face and the sadness transforms into brittle envy. "Never wanted to see me flourish!"

"Me?"

"Sabotaging my training from day one."

"Or you're not as shit hot as you might think."

125

"All right for you isn't it, not all of us had a rich mother croak, leave us a house! Talent's the only chance for us less fortunate than you to get out of toxic dead end fucking shit holes like this!" Alfie's face sinks. "And you nullified my talent. Which leaves me facing the grim reality of having to work those despicable strip club bogs once again. And for how long?"

"Still after all these years think I'm lucky."

Alfie slams on the breaks, fortunate that nobodies behind them to smash into his boot. "Nice little trek will teach you a bit about suffering. You fucking need it!"

"All right mate." Frankie slams the car door open and gets out, leaving it dangling in the road.

Alfie stretches over and pokes his head out of the passenger door as Frankie walks off. "Maybe we'll have this conversation again one day, with a bit more empathy involved ey!" His car screeches and smoke fumes from the tyres as he wizzes off.

Ten seconds later, a police car driven by Gavin hurtles past towards Alfie's car with its sirens blaring. Alfie pulls a handbrake turn into the other lane and speeds past Frankie, his back wheels slide on the damp road and his car skids passenger side on into a lamppost. Frankie sprints the short distance towards Alfie, a light dribble of blood flows from a cut on his scalp. His starry eyes are dazed, but he remains awake.

"Scuttle off boy," Alfie mutters as they share a brief, hostile stare down. "I'd rather die here than have you help me."

Gavin's whirling police car pulls up behind Alfie.

Frankie shrugs and walks off. "If you don't get sent down, have a brama one down the bogs."

As Frankie vanishes into the dimly lit back road's darkness, Gwyn and Gavin burst out of their car.

"Frank! You're our only witness," Gwyn shouts.

"Oi, get back here now!" Gavin screams, incensed by his costly decision of opting against having his dash cam fixed after it stopped working days ago – a mistake that will cost him a formal warning at the very least.

"Didn't see nothing me," Frankie says.

"Don't expect our co-operation when you need it lad," Gavin says with a callous look in his eye.

Despite being at least a seven-mile trek from here, Frankie's bubbling manic energy helps it feel possible, a feat his wobbly, ketamine-affected legs wouldn't have been able to fathom an hour ago. First village down as he powers through the windy run-down high street of Bethesda: chocker block with boarded-up old shops, the odd pub and masses of criminally unkempt flats for housing heroin and crack cocaine addicts. He struts past the Llangollen pub. Rambunctious Welsh-speaking drinkers fill up the pavement, struggling to keep themselves off the road. What Frankie would give for an extra quid in his pocket to add to his current GDP of £1.25 for a swift pint in a plastic glass for the walk. This establishment's firm policy of not selling half pints puts a stop to that.

Next comes the rough part as the adrenaline starts wearing off, a two-mile stretch of main road accompanied by a paper-thin pavement without street lights. Only a waist high, dry stone wall obstructs a grizzly steep drop down into a river via sharp mountain rocks sticking out of the ground. Piercing cold wind gusts him into the wall repeatedly and rattles the ancient trees stooping above the road. A boy racer ragging a white vintage Fiat Strada tears past Frankie at ninety miles an hour, knocking him off his feet backwards. Following closely behind, Alfie glares at Frankie from the backseat of Gavin's car that whizzes past at a far safer speed.

After an incident-free last mile stretch of darkness, he reaches the oasis of bright lampposts surrounding the tacky petrol garage and Little Chef combo and heads inside the messy, essentials-only garage. A miserable woman, overweight from her sedentary lifestyle and chocolate binge eating sessions, slouches out on her phone behind the counter, paying no attention to the shop. With his measly budget not stretching to afford even the simplest snack available – a sausage roll priced at an extortionate three pounds – he heads hesitantly to the till with it in hand. Despite noticing him with a restless glance upwards, the shop worker continues to scroll on Facebook for an awkward twenty seconds before putting the iPhone 3 down.

"It's all right if not, but would you let me pay for this another day, next time I come in?" Frankie quivers.

"Already done four statuses about your lot today," the shop cashier emphatically responds.

"I always come in here."

"Don't fucking tempt me into a fifth," Shop cashier says.

Frankie nods, resigned to his fate and strolls nonchalantly away.

"Food bank rat!" Shop cashier adds without looking up from her phone.

Frankie grits his teeth, notices the CCTV camera pointing slightly off centre and seizes the opportunity to pocket the sausage roll. He revels in the thought of the dismal women coughing up out of her own wages, something her stingy boss is notorious for enforcing. His own illicit use of the place for meetings with drug dealers mean there's a good chance the cameras aren't on anyway. Frankie wolfs down half of it in two bites once safely out of the shop's view, but hesitates before eating the rest. Knowing this was likely to be his only nourishment and stomach lining, he saves half for the last stretch of the walk, not wanting to have burnt the thing off before he reaches a mile from home. He struggles through the last few miles, the buzz from the beers and ketamine now replaced by a minor stitch.

With the wind and rain clattering down, he's happy to finally reach home. He lobs the sausage roll wrapper in next door's wide-open green wheelie bin, but misses and heads back to pick it up, placing it in the bin before confidently squaring into the house. Because he's back early, he has two blissful hours or so of peace ahead before Guy is bound to be back from pound a pint. Dazzler's illegally streaming Liverpool's FA cup third round replay against Wigan Athletic in the living room. With him being intensely engrossed in the game, Frankie doesn't even bother trying to say hello.

Suddenly Dazzler jumps up, effing and jeffing at images of Adrian, who's just made a howling error, allowing Wigan to equalize at one all. "Klopp man, get a keeper who can catch! Fuck sakes. Get out of my club Adrian, Wrexham are calling your name."

Frankie cracks open a stumpy bottle of brassiere beer, heads into the living room and shakes his head. "Don't tell me them wrong-un bookies have served you an acca again."

"Nah the sound lad got the sack. Bunch of miserable old Rudolphs in there now, all on their last warning for jarring on the job. Won't be taking chances like that, not any more. Good days are done for."

"Thank Christ for that!"

"Jonny's been on the withdrawals good and proper."

130

Frankie looks away with raised eyebrows as he swigs his beer.

"Will you do us dinner please Frank?"

Frankie sighs. "It's well late and I've eaten."

Dazzler's face sinks.

"Nothing left on the side when he pissed off out?" Frankie adds.

"Was there fuck. Lucozade diet today!"

Frankie grunts and storms into the kitchen. He opens the sticky, dishevelled fridge with its contents consisting of a meagre mouldy cling film-covered half an onion and an unwrapped half-empty packet of bacon. He carelessly squirts sunflower oil around the crusty communal frying pan without much due diligence.

"Didn't think about making this earlier?"

"Don't know how no?"

"Dingler of a bloke. Didn't watch that YouTube video I sent then?" Frankie restlessly says, with no response from Dazzler. "Piss easy it is Daz, come on man!"

"Bear can man!" Dazzler shouts in a shoddy Jamaican accent.

Frankie smiles, his guard broken as he swivels the pan around.

"This bacon bap, will go a long way towards my ambitions," Dazzler declares.

Frankie places the bacon rashers in the piping hot oil. "Oh yeah?"

"I've decided right. All I want is to be Bangor 1876's all-time great. That's it now," Dazzler defiantly says.

Frankie scoffs and takes a swig of beer.

"Three hundred bar a week you can get playing for them!" Dazzler defensively points out, offended by Frankie's seeming lack of belief in him.

"Phwoah, think big Les Davies will have a fair amount to say about that!"

Frankie puts together a three skinner spliff build before slapping together the sizzling bacon sandwich with Hovis thick-sliced white bread. Borderline undercooked, just as Dazzler likes it, a preference his body can hack after years of poorly-cooked food made with dirty pans around filthy kitchen surfaces. Frankie takes his weed stash out from under a floorboard and, with only a skinny joint's worth left kept aside from earlier despite stating the contrary to Byron, sleep will be hard to come by tonight. His usual bedtime spliff brims with at least a quarter of a gram.

Frankie hesitates remorsefully and takes a hefty first toke on his joint. "Daz, I've been sanctioned today I have."

"Oh yeah," Dazzler vacantly responds, knowing fully well what he means, knowledge about the world that would elude your average twelve-year-old.

"Might have to bail on the broadband for a bit." Frankie desperately sighs. "And I can't give you money for school no more."

"Fuck it! Venders, until they come out of the eighties, are a free-for-all! As is Old School's wallet when he hasn't pissed its content up the wall!"

Frankie chuckles while looking down.

"Give us a burn on that would you bruv?" Dazzler probes.

"You off your fucking head or what?"

"Hoping to be."

"You're twelve."

"Pain relief for the foot yeah, not to mention that crushing announcement of yours!" Frankie looks away, refusing to be coerced in the slightest. "Can't be arsed smoking another dimp joint man."

Frankie's eyes wildly whirl, he storms into the living room and tips the bustling ashtrays content into a makeshift carrier bag bin in the corner. "Do not smoke a dimp joint out of this room again! Promise me now!"

"Seen you do it down here, and in your room."

"Well if he's been seshing down here, which he has been, then you never fucking know what's gonna' be in them."

"Can't afford baccy unless Jonny and Wilder chip in for one!"

"Shit in there could fucking kill you if the wrong person's been here."

Frankie sighs, feeling empathy for Dazzler's plight having been there commonly himself since his early smoking days aged eleven. He throws a clump of five fags worth of tobacco on the table and heads back into the kitchen.

A foot high flame bellows up from the stove. "Shit!" Frankie rips the fire blanket off the wall by its mouldy dangling handle and smothers the flame, managing to quickly put it out. Dazzler strolls in and takes a worried look at Frankie who hangs his head shamefully.

Bereft of ideas and not up for robbing anything else tonight, Frankie heads half a mile down the road to Best Kebab Ye. A place that prides themselves on pleasing their regular loyal customers – certainly in comparison to their rival town centre kebab shops, who simply take the swathes of paralytic drinkers ordering donner meat and chips for granted. Frankie hesitantly heads in. Its tiny compact waiting area is surrounded by bright, vibrant Hindu decorations. A drunk couple with gothic long black hair moider brashly while waiting for their food. An expressionless bald delivery driver, known for taking sickies off work when out of weed stands in the corner, stoned of his mind, holding a hefty delivery hot bag.

"Naboo mate, how's it going?" Frankie says.

A tall Indian man wearing a stylish white and black striped Yves Saint Laurent polo shirt turns around. Being a true one-man army, he doesn't trust anyone else to uphold his high standards in the food preparation department. "Oi oi Frank." He frantically drops baskets of chips into the deep fat fryer and shaves off lamb donner meat. "What you having boss?"

"Look, you know me. Have a situation at home I have. Couldn't do us a couple of meals on tick could you please? Literally anything."

Naboo looks down and leans on the counter. "I've always thought you're good lad, I like you, and your brother. Proper characters yeah. But is any of it for--" He sighs. "I apologize to say it like this, but that scumbag prick old man of yours?"

"You have my word."

Naboo nods and gets to work, starting off by throwing a generous handful of chips into the fryer and sticking four large beef patties on the grill. Frankie sits down, overwhelmed by the relief flowing through his veins. He thoroughly looks forward to what will be his first takeaway for over two months, a luxury given that his dole payments go on weed, tobacco, Dazzler's school money and cheap supermarket food with whatever is left. A twenty-minute wait flies by owing to the manic thoughts from his gargantuan day. For once, he feels proud of himself. Proud of standing up to the overbearing demands of Alfie that he's long grown tired of, having always been fearful of calling out his only friend at the time. His newly found friendship with Damo and Byron ensures that's no longer the case. He picks up the two-stacked double layered paper bags of takeaway food, not knowing what's in them, and thanks Naboo profusely. So much so, that he annoyingly blocks the ever-expanding cue of punters and heads out proudly into the street with his head held high.

While taking a break from drinking to sell a bag of cocaine to a punter too anxious to be within eye sight of the pub, Damo and Byron sneak up behind Frankie. Startling him enough to nearly drop the food.

"Look who it is!" Damo sarcastically says.

"Money for takeaway, money for snooker." Byron inspects the size of the bags.

"Happy for us to buy you jars all night though weren't you?" Damo tears the top off one of the bags and looks inside, beaming as he turns away. "Fucking feast and a half he's got there."

"All free," Frankie mumbles.

Byron and Damo gaze at each other with wry smirks and sarcastically nod.

"Oh yeah, all right then mate," Byron says.

"I swear!" Frankie insists.

Damo snatches both bags off Frankie who barely resists, him and Byron strut off proudly. Frankie stands rooted to the spot, stunned to the core. He sheds a single tear and Damo swiftly returns, cynically cackling as he hands Frankie the bags back.

"I'm not gonna' take your food lad!" Damo howls at Frankie's continued distress, who eventually half-heartedly side smiles. "Few jars again soon?"

Frankie's eyes light up. "On me next time."

Damo winks and walks off chuckling. Being familiar to cynical behavior for laughs at his own expense, Frankie doesn't think much of it.

Frankie dumps the food bags on the table in front a stunned Dazzler. They collectively unearth their family feast of two half-pound special donner meat burgers, three large chips, two chicken donner kebab wraps, a ten-inch meat feast pizza with onion and a one-and-a-half-litre bottle of Pepsi Max. Having no issue munching through the lot, bar a portion of chips and the last slice of pizza. Frankie manages to sink all but one of his six pack of stumpy beers in the forty odd minutes taken to conquer their food mountain. After a few episodes of Family Guy repeats on BBC3, Frankie drifts off in a comatose state. Dazzler stealthily takes a pinch from his tobacco pouch before sneaking off upstairs.

A few hours later, just when getting into a deep sleep, the front door slams shut. While this only partially awakens Frankie, Guy rushing in, gurning and shaking him completes the job.

"Wake up boy. Wake up!" Guy urgently says.

Frankie flails his arms around wildly trying to push Guy away. After failing in his attempt, he stuffs a cushion over his head.

"Piss off!" Frankie shouts. Guy continues shaking him, progressively vigorously, with sturdy determination. "Give me a fucking second."

"Get up now," Guy insists.

Frankie begrudgingly sits up and lights a half-smoked joint propped up in the ashtray. Guy fiercely clenches his fists and grits his teeth.

"You two little toe rags have some nerve." Guy slaps Frankie across his chin, sending his joint flying across the room, a mini cut opens up on his lower lip. "Fucking takeaway in my house, without me? I'm ashamed, ashamed of the greed that gushes within you both. I really am."

Undeterred, Frankie gets up in Guy's face. "Best thing you can do is keep doing what you're doing old man, keep it up! Gives us every chance of being nothing like--"

Guy leathers Frankie one on the mouth with a closed fist and a front tooth of Frankie's cracks jaggedly without his head moving. He remains transfixed to Guy. Not for long however, as Guy lands a right hook flush on Frankie's temple, sending him staggering back into a loose pile of DVDS, only holding himself up with the corners of the walls. Guy pounces and grabs him by the scruff of the neck with his left hand, walloping him six times. Dazzler appears and jumps up on Guy's neck from behind, locking his arms around Guy's flabby turkey neck and wrapping his legs around Guys waist, utilizing jiu-jitsu tips picked up from endless Saturday nights streaming Las Vegas UFC cards. Guy waves his head around violently, unable to quite shake Dazzler off. With time to partially recover, Frankie staggers back up to his feet. With his left eye now totally swollen shut, he uppercuts Guy right in the balls which knocks the wind clean out of him. Guy pants desperately as Frankie lands an identical shot on his testes, only this time twice as hard. Guy staggers to his knees, then to his side, with Dazzler managing to keep hold of Guy the entire time, despite cutting his forehead on the floor as they flop over sideways. He tightens his grip on the choke and holds it until Guy's unconscious, then gets straight up, gazes at Frankie's battered and bruised face and tightly hugs his brother.

Frankie breaks off and stamps on Guy's head. "What!"

Dazzler tries to restrain Frankie, which is ferociously resisted. "It's not worth it."

"He's had his fucking day."

"Get sent down and I really will be alone."

After a few seconds the magnitude of Dazzler's statement dawns large and he ceases to resist, opting instead to spit blood and a shard of his tooth at Guy's head. Frankie picks the joint up off the floor and staggers towards the garden door, slouching on the frame as he sparks up the joint. After quickly losing his footing, he falls head first onto the garden's gravel floor.

Frankie wakes up to being strapped onto a stretcher firmly by Keith, a stressed-out paramedic in his fifties desperately awaiting retirement. He peeks around nervously.

"You're all right lad, cops have had him, just stay where you are," Keith says, devoid of emotion from being institutionalized in his job out of fear of not being able to afford cocaine should he quit.

Frankie looks up to see Twiggy on the other side of the stretcher, nicknamed as you'd expect because of his skinny stature, who's absolutely bricking himself. Being new to the medical field, this is the gnarliest situation his inaugural two months in the service has thrown his way.

"Ready?" Keith sternly says, far from showing any belief in the rookie opposite him. They brace themselves to lift the stretcher and as it's hoisted up, Twiggy lifts sideways at the wrong angle, leaving Frankie perilously off balance.

"Daliai cont!" They place the stretcher down. Keith turns red in the face. "Stoned gach yn gwaith eto. Ffocin nobed. Ffwc ti meddwl wti. Hamro vallys yn gwaith. Diawl o foi!"

"Dio ddim yr amser I prygethu!" Twiggy insists as Frankie fades out of consciousness.

Chapter 7 - Bryn Y Neuadd

Frankie's following few months proved harrowing to say the least. Briefly, he blissfully had the house to himself following his father's horrific assault and subsequent three-year prison sentence, two years for the assault and one for child negligence. However, given his traumatic head injuries and the nasty vertigo that lingered alongside, he was vulnerable and unable to always fully look after himself. With Dazzler sent immediately to Bryn Y Neuadd care home following the assault, where he's languished ever since, Damo and Byron stepped in to help, a seemingly noble gesture at the time. They took his shopping lists to Lidl, got him whatever was required and kept him company with what started off as an innocent twice weekly session on the gear and beers. Gradually they were popping over in the mornings for swift blitzes of weighing and packaging bags of cocaine and ketamine, claiming to be worried about leaving the traces of evidence at their own place. Frankie's unspoken reservations were nipped in the bud and numbed by the occasional weed handout, between half and a full gram on occasions to smoke as a reward. This progressed over the coming weeks, and the courtesy of checking with Frankie before turning up diminished – with them now rocking up at all times of the night, even going as far as stealthily breaking the back door's lock without Frankie noticing as to further convenience their regular coming and going. Over time, this absolutely shattered the shed's tarpaulin roof after having them hop over the wall onto it continuously. Their friendliness as well as consent drastically dwindled after a month or so. Progressively, they made Frankie increasingly uncomfortable and started banishing him to his room unless they wanted something.

Then the parties started as well as the presence of the halfway house rogues. Derfel and Ali in particular became regular fixtures, both favouring the spacious living room that they were making their own over the small rooms and shabby halfway house courtyard. Such was the hostility thrown his way when cooking food in the open plan kitchen and living room, Frankie's weight plummeted despite him already being dangerously skinny. After being dished out final warnings at the halfway house, it became Byron and Damo's dealing spot. They even went as far as placing a knife on a neighbour's throat, to punish their audacity of complaining about the rowdy customers shouting outside when turning up without prior appointment. Dazzler's room became the designated shagging room, for when brave women that dared enter what had become even more of a shit hole. Personified by the thriving rat community making themselves at home in the yard's stray bin bags, often Frankie's room for cover during storms. What solidified the

142

house's status as a trap house, and brought order to proceedings, was the release from prison of the fierce Wrexham dealer Konrad Clark, fresh from serving a five-year sentence for cocaine dealing. A feared ex-drug enforcer turned dealer, he serves as Byron and Damo's line manager and identified the place as the new base of his county lines operation. Frankie's reward for keeping quiet progressed to a strip of Valium and a twenty bag of weed a week, feeding his ever-increasing drug addiction.

Frankie lies belly down on a grubby, sheetless, springy mattress under a coverless, musty duvet, now far paler and gaunt in appearance owing to his ever-increasing ketamine, Valium and alcohol abuse. After being rudely awoken by rumbling and shouting from downstairs, he looks up at his bare, furniture-shy room containing only a telly and a small pile of clothing. Empty Valium packets, revolting ash trays and cans of value lager litter the dusty, sticky carpet and surfaces. A DVD case with skeletons of last night's bedtime ketamine lines and a rolled-up train ticket lies nearby. His vision sparkles from dehydration as he reaches over to grab a Valium strip and tobacco from the floor, necking a Valium in an instant and washing it down with dregs of a Galleryx beer.

After multiple spates of rage following consecutive significant drug losses owing to their incompetence, Frankie's now dishevelled living room wall's plastered with punched-in holes. One of the culprits of such brute force, Konrad, is sat with Byron weighing and bagging one-gram bags of ketamine. His large frame and puffy Canada Goose jacket squashes Byron into the armrest of the torn and tattered two-seat sofa.

"Don't be ticking flat out this time Wee wee lad, this is far from clown grade MXE," Konrad warns.

This is Byron's first opportunity to prove himself as more than just a runner, following consecutive atrocious quarterly financial performances owing to his tentative approach to debt retrieval.

"I always get it back me," Byron lies, dismayed at having his incompetence called out in front of Damo, whose rivalry to be the highest earner with has intensified.

Damo scoffs from the other side of the room where he stirs ketamine in a saucepan with a spatula, wearing a clean beige apron. "First thing a crusty wreck head round here thinks when they want a bit of free gear, is get that drip Byron 'Three to one' Wee wee on the blower," he mockingly says. "That being the odds on the street of having to pay a Wee wee tick."

Byron grunts and aggressively bags a gram of ketamine up with a bitchy scowl on his face. "Prick," he mutters as he grabs two nos canisters out of a box.

Konrad spots this and, determined not to miss out on the fun, grabs four.

"Don't hammer them no." Byron's resentment stems from being the only one who's chipped in on nos for months, with the others knowing it'll be about owing to Byron's ever-increasing reliance on it.

Konrad lobs two canisters at Damo, one hits him on the back of the head and the other lands in the brewing ketamine. Damo turns around and smirks sarcastically.

"Get them down you bum boy!" Konrad chants.

Having bucked up the courage to head downstairs and face the day, Frankie takes a pee in his bedroom sink while smoking a fag, wincing as the pain of his ketamine induced bladder infection takes hold. As his lightbulb flickers on and off, he throws in the plug and fills up the sink basin. He grunts when realizing it's been done in the wrong order, and will now be washing his face out of the freshly pissed-in sink. Knowing the bathroom sink is blocked with projectile vomit after last night, he bites the bullet and splashes his face in his own pissy sink, freshening up as sharply as the grim facilities and facial wash lotion rationing can make him. He ventures out into the hallway, flickering on the light only to

145

remember Konrad swinging on the light socket, imitating a chimpanzee and pulling it clean out of the roof the night before. This adds peril to the walk downstairs given the near permanent scattering of broken glass occupying the floor. He tiptoes down the stairs, tripping towards the bottom on a lifeless women sprawled out on the floor.

Konrad sucks a nos balloon into his lungs with all the power his diaphragm can withstand.

"Won't do nos because he's a vegan." Byron scrunches his face in disbelief.

Damo shrugs and turns his attention back to the simmering ketamine on the stove.

"Biggest fucking gimp going. You'll be right on the beek later, and I'm telling you now that's not even in the same stratosphere as vegan lad," Byron adds.

Frankie stumbles backwards through the door with his hands up defensively, cutting Byron off. A scatty women in her twenties, Dolly, an occasional prostitute and the group's pass-around shag, slaps Frankie with open palms around the head repeatedly with sinister intent.

"Fuck do you think you are, wasting my hit!" Dolly shrieks, distraught at having been woken up at the peak of her heroin trip.

Konrad spits out his balloon such is the ferocity of his chilling laughter. Frankie pins Dolly against the wall with his forearm, holding his free arm up as a clenched fist.

146

"Fucking give me ten bar now!" Dolly insists.

"You passed out on the stairs, and I didn't see you. That's all there is to it." Frankie lets go of Dolly after a few tense seconds, she immediately phlegms in his face.

"I'll get it off you." Dolly passes by and takes a seat in the living room with a wry smirk slapped on her face. Byron and Konrad howl in laughter, barely able to control themselves.

"Touch me again. Bird or not." Frankie fiercely wipes the spit off his face.

Konrad's amusement abruptly ends. "Well it's thirty bar off you every day she's a bit too *knocked out* to partake, my mate."

Frankie looks down powerlessly at his feet. Owing thirty pounds a day that he simply doesn't have could lead to being forced into all sorts of favours, perhaps violent, or even having to taking a hefty package of vallies into prison – all things he's been threatened with in the past. Through careful avoidance of debt, he's swerved these consequences as of yet. He heads over to the fridge and takes out a fresh carton of eggs and a packet of bacon.

"Who let him put them in there?!" Konrad storms over to Frankie and snatches the eggs. "No eggs in my office. I fucking told you that! Didn't I tell him that?" Konrad pelts the eggs into the bin.

Frankie hastily grabs out a frying pan and squirts oil around it.

"And you're not frying fuck all, not while that vegan nonce cooks our gear. Get it away, now!" Konrad melodramatically says.

Get the grill on lad, plenty of space over here." Damo creepily ushers him over.

Frankie bends down, opens the oven door and Damo bends down behind him. "Long as you don't mind me being nosey." He whispers in Frankie's ear while tightly grabbing his buttock.

Frankie jolts up and spends the bacon's cooking time out in the yard smoking, trying with all his might to withhold tears. Despite the less than favourable treatment of him by this motley crew, never has he felt as unsafe and violated by any of them. With the bacon only partly cooked, Frankie sticks it on a plate with shaky hands and rushes up the stairs to a chorus of chuckles while everyone revels in his discomfort. With his appetite well and truly scuppered, Frankie lets it all out and sobs profusely, heading straight for his ketamine stash. He sits back on his bed, crushes a three-inch sized line with a five-pound note and credit card on his phone case before devouring the lot in one sitting. Lying back in his new found peace, a trickle of blood drips out of his nose.

Jonny leads the determined quartet of himself, Dazzler, Wilder, and the school's tag-along class clown Mcoley as they peg it towards Morrison's on push bikes. All having left school at lunch time to dodge double French lessons. Jonny power slides across the final stretch, narrowly avoiding a few disgruntled pensioners. Mcoley lags behind and arrives later than the rest, his hundred kilo frame on a twelve year old's body unable to keep up.

Dazzler and Jonny grab a basket, neither bearing any intention of using them, but both take shoplifting seriously and understand that every step in appearing a legitimate customer matters. Dazzler and Wilder form one pre-determined pairing, with the thinking that with Mcoley being a relative shoplifting novice, the vastly experienced Jonny will dig them out of any tight spots should they arise. Dazzler heads for the bakery section and crouches by the counter with a rucksack on his back. He's borrowing Wilder's on account of his comparative lightning speed, therefore adequately equipped to escape with their haul. Wilder diligently checks their path right and left, unzips the rucksack and stuffs it chocker block full of white chocolate cookies, custard doughnuts and packs of steak pies. Over on chocolate duty in the treats aisle, Mcoley brazenly grabs handful of bars, erratically stuffing them into Jonny's rucksack, the pressure evidently proving tough for him to handle.

"Composure!" Jonny sharply says while picking up multipacks of Snickers dropped on the floor.

Dazzler and Wilder sneak over to the usual escape pod of the lift down into the car park, where a pre-planned pinpointed pathway through isn't covered by CCTV. A disaster, the lift won't respond and Dazzler's bashing of the button catches the attention of the comically short security guard. So the boys dart off towards the exit, alerting Jonny and Mcoley on the way. Dazzler, Jonny and Wilder get away in enough time to fly off on their bikes and evade the hapless security guard, who's now joined in his pursuit by a chunkier colleague. Mcoley however, is let down once again by his brittle mobility as the larger security guard bashes his mountain bike away and restrains him with no issues.

"Get off me man!" Mcoley shouts. Out comes the panting smaller security guard, he rips the bag out of Mcoley's hands after some savage rugby maul type resistance from the promising Bangor rugby club under thirteen's hooker. A rough night down the cop shop awaits poor Mcoley, and with this being his fourth misdemeanor of the year, so does an odds on chance of a short stretch at borstal. Not that he'll be overly bothered, Bryn Y Neuadd care home isn't any more prosperous and the food can't be worse in jail.

Jonny, Wilder and Dazzler race back to the care home for what will be Wilder's introduction to the place's notoriously fowl grub on his first day. Jeff 'brick', his single parent father, had somehow evaded social services all these years, despite his drug addiction-induced neglectful parenting. Only reaching his respective final straw in losing custody after being sentenced to two years inside for selling just enough heroin to fund his own habit. Taking the blame bagged him an extra year inside, fearful of the repercussions should he mention Konrad as his supplier. They're joined at the table by the only other two residents, Felix and Brenda, both veterans of the care home circuit, fourteen and nearing the magic age of sixteen when they'll inevitably be cut off from the support afforded to them by the system. Small bits of bacon, runny mash potato and salad leaves bearing an off-putting shade of green shape up Paul Chef's choice of cuisine for the evening. A collective air of apprehension dominates the room as everyone other than Jonny struggles to swallow the dismal food. A bit of Wilder's half frozen bacon proves tough to cut up. Jonny wolfs his food down with no issue, while Felix and Brenda have had enough. Despite burning hunger pains, they spit out their mouthfuls and Dazzler follows their lead by doing the same.

"Don't half dish out turd when the new lads rock up," Brenda bitterly says, glaring at Wilder as she pushes her plate away.

"Jonny doesn't care though no?" Felix says.

Jonny adamantly shakes his head. "After many years of getting fuck all. Four, five, six days on the trot." His face lights up. "I'll scran anything me. Frozen or not." Jonny unapologetically stuffs a mouthful of food in his mouth.

"Specs lad, we're brimming with top draw consumables. And you're choosing to munch that shit?" Dazzler points out.

Jonny spits out the food. "Spot on our Dazzler. Save the runs and food poisoning for a rainy day, I like your style!" He shoves the plate away.

"My bag head old man rustled up finer grub," Wilder says with a grimace.

Felix, Jonny, Dazzler and Brenda gaze anxiously towards the door as the home's sinister, sadistic lead carer Ben sneaks in and rolls up his button up shirtsleeves.

"Tripping off his nutsack." Wilder's cut off from telling his story by Ben grabbing his hair from behind and shoving his face downwards into the food.

"Pity all he feels like doing is smashing scag and chugging Strongbow all day then isn't it?" Ben says in Wilder's ear before letting go of him.

Wilder pants for air and glowers at Ben. Dazzler puffs out his chest and gets out of his seat. Felix restrains him, fearing for the inevitable group consequences already coming their way for attempted violence.

"So do yourself a favour and learn some fucking respect, be grateful for what you're given." Ben glares at everyone individually before fixating on the irate Dazzler. "The lot of you."

Ben smirks as he heads out the room. Wilder furiously wipes the food off his face with an already dirtied napkin, lights a pre-rolled fag and storms out into the yard. Felix storms off, dismayed by the new kid's dissent that will cost them all dearly. Not only will they now be cooked the same drivel for the next few dinners, despite the catering company possessing far tastier options, but their measly five pound a week pocket money will no doubt be scaled down or withheld entirely. Ben runs this place like a military camp and it's known as the second worst care home in the area, with the worst, nicknamed Saville block on Anglesey, being rife with sexual abuse. A lingering threat of being sent there is Ben's way of trying to keep everyone in line. Having seen swathes of his friends sent there over the years and never being the same again after, Felix harbours a plan to punish Wilder. With the consent of Ben, who gladly complies, Felix and Brenda get themselves locked in the TV room alone with Wilder, hoping to dish him out a right kicking. However, this backfires as the seemingly soft-looking Wilder flattens Felix with his first punch. Having been taught not to hit women, he holds his fist up at Brenda, but without the assistance of her trusty sidekick, she bricks it and slams on the locked door until Ben lets her out. Threatened by Wilder's defiance to these anarchic, military forms of control,

Ben immediately books Wilder's place in Saville block. With the plan being that he'll be transferred over in four days' time, Ben decides not to tell Wilder until an hour before he leaves.

Gwyn and Gavin arrive at the door. Not being after an arrest, they simply want a word at the end of their shift after being told of Dazzler, Jonny, and Wilder's shoplifting antics. They pelt the doorbell and Ben races to answer, opening the door with a grizzly, unwelcoming scowl.

"Sorry to bother you Ben, but two of your new lads, Dazzler and--" Gwyn says.

"Wilder!" Gavin emphatically adds, finishing off Gwyn's quivering sentence. "And Jon specs. All of them, been copped on CCTV grafting a whole load of stock down Morrisons."

Ben grimaces, looks down and ushers the coppers in. "I'll lead you right to the thieving little fucks! Nothing but grief they've been for me."

"Given their.. recent collective bad luck--" Gwyn carefully chooses his words.

"No little terror here hides behind any of that," Ben insists.

Gavin looks on in awe, subtly nodding.

"Ok. Provided I can have chat with them, I'm willing to turn a blind eye. For this to be treated as their final warning," Gwyn softly suggests.

"That's all you're here for? A half-arsed dressing down from a pair of shitbag clowns? Be honest with you, I'll do a far fucking better job of that," Ben claims.

"Ok, Ben, we'll--" Ben slams the door shut in their face. "Leave you to it."

Dazzler lies on his mattress, barely elevated off the floor. His musty room's window frame's covered in built up condensation mould. He grinds up some weed, acquired on tick at school by a scrawny kid in the year above that Dazzler has no desire to pay the following day as agreed. Suddenly the doorknob creaks, Dazzler panics, hides all of his smoking equipment under the pillow and stands up straight, ready for action, only being afforded the time to do so through Ben's momentary struggle to open the stiff door.

"So where is it all then?" Ben clinically asks.

"All of what?" Dazzler neutrally replies.

"Just had the coppers here for you, I think you know why!" Ben shouts, shattering his short-lived attempt at remaining calm.

Dazzler belatedly shrugs, taken aback by Ben's ferocity. Ben regimentally bashes everything off the shelves, including Dazzler's TV and Xbox 360, finishing off by tipping out the content of Dazzler's black bags. Distraught at not finding what he was after, Ben looks around guiltily, even for his own harsh standards knowing he's gone a tad too far this time.

Ben bitterly turns to Dazzler. "You and that trampy little fuck Wilder are gone, out of here. Already bagged him a spot in Llangefni, just you wait until they have space for you."

"Get the stumpies out then why don't you," Dazzler coldly says, masking his overwhelming inner fear.

Ben goes viciously red in the face and throws Dazzler onto the bed. Grimacing as he holds his head in his hands and looks around the trashed room and cracked TV screen. Unable to take the sight any longer, he abruptly leaves.

That was it for Wilder, too tough for his own good and posing a threat to Ben's authority, he was duly shipped out to fend for himself. Most likely, he'd be all right given his ability to fight, but the threat of sexual abuse from caregivers will always loom large. Although it took four days instead of one to get him there, much to Ben's dismay. To keep him out of the way in the meantime, each of those were spent cleaning Ben's four-bedroom detached country house after blagging the school to sign Wilder off sick. Bogus claims he had Covid was Ben's excuse, something his supposed prestige allowed him to do, without sending proof of a positive test to the school's medical department.

Chapter 8 - Passing the buck

On a highly anticipated Wednesday night, Konrad, Byron, and Damo enjoy a few pre-drinks in the living room while playing FIFA for a pound a game. Suffering from a horrendous comedown having smoked thirty pounds worth of crack last night, Dolly flops in through the back door. This stuns Frankie who's making toast, the first thing he's had the courage to get up and make all day. Dolly's in tears, partly due to her ravenous cravings, but also because of feeling sorry for herself having just cancelled a twenty-pound, fifteen minute long booking to give one her regulars on AdultWork a blowjob. A move that'll no doubt harm her reputation and give an advantage to Tilly Lick, her fierce local competitor, who joins her in the category of having one of the county's cheapest rates on the site.

"Nah, no more tick. Piss off," Konrad says the second he spots her.

"C'mon, don't be sly, for fucking once," Dolly splutters, perching down distressingly on her knees facing Konrad, much to Byron and Damo's amusement.

"Get out there slagging, and you'll be back here in an hour," Konrad pedantically says.

"I need a taste before I can face it!"

"Can't hack the comedown without scag, well fucking don't get down a oner with me."

Dolly lays her head on Konrad's lap, drenching his new maroon red Adidas tracksuit bottoms with tears and chemical-ridden sweat. "I'll fuck you all night Keez, you know I will."

Konrad shoves Dolly away deliberately in Damo's direction. Such is his shock, he drops the controller. "Don't you touch me!" He forcefully shoves her onto the floor and wrings his hands out. She lies there flopped out and sniffling in defeat.

"Shag-for-scag went out the window the moment you got Hep C Dol!" Konrad mockingly claims.

Byron celebrates a goal by Dominic Calvert-Lewin despite having had the advantage of Damo dropping the controller and allowing him through on goal.

"Her fault that was! No chance you're getting a quid if I lose," Damo defiantly declares.

Frankie's white bread toast pops out of the toaster, he picks it up with his trembling hand and sticks it on a plate to leave. Too nervous to stick around long enough to butter it.

Dolly grabs Frankie's crotch from behind. "Ain't forgotten that tenner." She whispers seductively in his ear before kissing him repeatedly on the neck.

With his free arm, Frankie backward elbows Dolly in the face, sending her clattering to the floor. He drops the plate of toast and looks nervously over at Konrad, awaiting his fate.

"Long as she buys a bit of gear tomorrow," Konrad says without looking up from the chunky lines of cocaine he's racking up.

Content with his conditional reprieve, Frankie darts upstairs, putting aside his lingering hunger for the time being, until the house is empty in a few hours at least. It proves to be a struggle as the hours slither by and it reaches 10 PM without them yet having trudged off for their weekly fill of borderline expired Carlsberg. So much so, that Frankie decides to doze off early to conquer the hunger, a tactic mastered in his early life when having to cope on many occasions without dinner.

After a mere haze of light sleep, he's rudely awakened by loud kicking and thumping of the front door. Small chippings off the house's wall are pelted up against Frankie's window like missiles. After a few seconds he wakes up in a daze having pissed himself once again. He peeks under the sheets before sneaking over to the window. Keiran, Byron and Damo glare up at him.

"Open it you goose neck prick! What you locking the back for?" Konrad shouts up, slurring his words.

Frankie sprints over to the table, grabs a key, drops it out of the window and falls back into bed, covering himself up tightly. He shudders as the front door is thrust open, clearly audible with it being directly under his room, followed by the crack of it shutting. A non-violent screeching debate between Damo and Keiran muffles through the floorboards. With Damo stating his case as to how preposterous the awarding to Qatar to host the 2022 World Cup is given their stance on criminalizing homosexuality. This is soon drowned out by a generic late 2010's trap beat. A piece of cutlery in a bowl shakes such is the power of the speaker's bass from downstairs. Frankie checks his phone, which states 6 AM. Knowing his chances of sleeping away the trembling hunger are done for, he sits up miserably, licks a rizla and makes an L shaped build for a morning hash spliff. Its nicotine hit does nothing to stifle his hunger, and he makes the tough decision to venture downstairs to try and eat, once his depleted body finds the energy to rise.

Damo racks up a half gram line of ketamine having been starved of anything but a few small keys while out. Under Konrad's strict instructions, both him and Byron were warned not to take more than a small personal amount to the pub owing to their ever-increasing notoriety. What Konrad deems a personal amount barely touches Damo's high tolerance sides. After smashing half of the line, he splutters before the end and can't finish it, sinking back into the sofa lifelessly with his eyes drooped open. Konrad holds his phone camera

160

up, ready to record one of his lauded Snapchat videos, he's gurning, sweating and his pupils are almost sunk back into his head.

"Day fucking three of." Konrad snorts a line of speed off a plate, the one drug guaranteed to send him loopy, sometimes while on it, almost always the day after. His head twitches, the sting of his knackered right nostril's hard to hide. He waves the camera in Damo's vacant face. "Well, not for Mr 'I've never been in a k hole me' Hayward." He pans the camera over to the half-finished line and crusty rolled up twenty-pound note alongside, before picking up a stray can of beer and pouring a few swigs worth over Damo's face. There's no reaction. "Thought you benders had a bit of sesh in you, man." Konrad pours a larger amount directly down Damo's throat and chuckles as Damo gags, but still doesn't wake up.

Bored by Damo's comatose state, Konrad sticks the camera in Byron's sweaty face, who's stood up raving on the spot to 'Sigma – I know' that's blaring off the telly on FreeView's 4Music.

"As brama as a tune could ever be," Byron passionately claims with his beady eyes glued to the TV.

Frankie skulking into the kitchen lethargically grabs Konrad's attention.

"No way boys, goose neck's on the sesh." Konrad stuffs the camera in Frankie's face until he's cowering in the corner of the kitchen.

Back up the stairs Frankie goes, only once Konrad has had enough footage for his sesh montage of course. With no chance of grabbing anything from the kitchen, he painstakingly waits it out for the four-hour gap before his visit with Dazzler – a quick joint on Bangor Mountain before school. Frankie has no-showed to the last few after necking inordinate amounts of Valium and being unable to hear his alarm, so this one is crucial to uphold in order to maintain some sort of trust.

With a collection of rusty small change, mostly coppers, Frankie treats himself to a thirty pence half-sized white baguette from Morrisons en route, wolfing half of it down before even reaching the shop's entrance. He attempts a no-look throw of the baguette's wrapper into a nearby bin, and despite noticing it miss, doesn't go and pick it up. He stumbles down the last stretch of the journey, a poorly maintained, nettle-infested downward mountain path, one of the premium heroin shooting and dealing spots in town. Dazzler's already at the bottom, sat on step smoking a fag, he raises his hand lopsidedly at Frankie.

"How are you scrapper lad?" Frankie cautiously says, alarmed at the marks on Dazzler's face.

"Should've seen the state he was in!" Dazzler bullishly responds. Frankie tries to conceal a grin. "Joss gave you worse anyway."

"Detached fucking retina man." Frankie points to his right eye.

Dazzler sarcastically puffs out his chest and puts on Guy's Kent accent. "Well, you robbed her ten out of ten cally boy, three weeks to ship more of that over. Any mother would've done the same." They both burst out laughing.

"Worth it for the month off school alone," Frankie emphatically claims. Dazzler's lighter buckles while lighting his fag and Frankie lights both his and his own. "Surprised you're out of bed lad."

"Says the one! Looks like you're still in bed. Proper grim one at that," Dazzler bitterly remarks, triggered by his brother's ribbing. A brief awkward silence falls between them. "That Rudolph cunt down there had me and Wilder fucking weeding and scrubbing bogs. Half six!"

Frankie grimaces and chucks a chunky bud in his grinder. "Still giving you grief?"

"Much as I let him." Dazzler turns away and sheds a tear out of Frankie's view, swiftly wiping it away and putting on a forced smile. "Be sweet if I could just come back home though wouldn't it?"

"Oh, any week now mate," Frankie confidently claims. Dazzler's eyes perk up. "One or two things to sort out."

As soon as it's lifted, Dazzler's face sinks once again, a classic Frankie excuse of the last few months, a sure sign of absolutely zilch happening.

"One of them being fibre optic for the Liverpool West Ham semi-final, and, the IPL double header after it." Frankie struggles to roll the joint.

Dazzler looks away in dismay.

Heard that one before mate.

Later that evening, Frankie's on his usual pre-party delivery services for the crew. While stood bashfully in front of them in the living room, Konrad, Damo and Byron throw money at him. Dolly lies with her legs up on the sofa, dissociating, having managed to overcome her earlier meltdown to get out and fulfill a quick fifteen minute appointment. Ash from her lit fag flickers off the end and burns holes in her black tights.

"Get us nine twenty crates of skippies aye, and err, fockin' steak burgers." Konrad throws an extra fiver at Frankie.

"Pink gin with my twenty, I ain't chipping in on no skippies man," Damo assertively says.

"Awkward cunt, fifty bar for nine crates," Konrad says.

Damo shrugs with a sadistic grin.

"You and your pink gin man!" Konrad screeches and looks down, embarrassed by his mini-meltdown.

Frankie scrambles around picking up the mixture of change and notes off the floor. "I'll get what I can."

Dolly snaps back into full consciousness, shakes Byron's shoulder and asks in his ear; "Is he going shop?"

"Yeah." Byron winces, pushes her away and lobs a pound coin that hits Frankie on the side of the head. "Get this one some fucking airwaves."

Dolly falls off the sofa, such is her urgency to grab a small duffel bag behind it. "Change that for a score while you're at it." She pulls out a filthy carrier bag absolutely stacked with twenty pounds worth of small value dirty coins.

Frankie gags at the rusty whiff coming from the bag and chucks it on the table. "Piss right off."

Dolly erupts and aims a kick at Frankie's calf which misses as he heads for the front door.

"Oi!" Konrad shouts just as Frankie has his hands on the door handle, his deep angry voice ripples through the wall separating them that he thumps repeatedly. "Be nothing here waiting for you if you don't."

Panic stations set in, given the predominant reason for being so willing to fulfill this errand is to secure something to help him sleep through the party. "Since when have I had to do favours for the weekly strip!"

After getting no answer, Frankie storms back into the living room and takes the filthy bag with him.

Muddy from the walk and treading filth up the Tesco Extra store's floor, Frankie picks up the last nine crates of stumpies – avoiding what would have been a guaranteed night without the Valium had he come back empty handed.

He loads the crates, gin and burgers onto checkout three, as specified by Konrad and tips the change from the carrier bag onto the counter.

"Change this for me please?" He asks the pale, ragged checkout server.

"Konrad!" She grits her teeth, having been pulled this trick on by him on multiple occasions for being one day late on a fifty-pound cocaine tick. She glares up at Frankie.

"Twenty squids there," Frankie says.

She soon realizes the repercussions should she not do the favour. Without doubt, her bags will be dipped by 0.2 of a gram at the very least. She checks the empty cue behind Frankie. "Never again mate." She pedantically slips on a pair of disposable gloves.

Frankie rubs his hands on his face in relief and gets on the phone to Klaus' Cabs – a local criminal front taxi company – while he waits. Only to be told their rates have risen and will now cost him four pound fifty to get home, which to his dismay leaves him short.

With no security guard on the door tonight, Frankie's path's clear to nab the trolley and wheel it home, proving troublesome in the boggy pavement-less main road on

166

route. His only scare was an upcoming cop car, which Frankie dealt with by shoving the trolley in a nearby bush, leaving enough time to avoid detection as it hurtled past.

From virtually the second he opens the door, the trolley's pulled ferociously into the living room. Frankie stuffs a twenty-pound note into Dolly's chest, not giving her the chance to get any closer to him than is necessary. Byron and Damo gleefully grab their drinks, with Damo particularly enthralled. Not surprising, having barred himself from drinking for a week in attempt to wean his dependence off it. A landmark moment in his adult life, the first week since the age of thirteen without drinking, with that including home brew during his prison sentences. Konrad however, is more excited by the boastful spew he's chatting to Glesni and Delyth, who arrived minutes earlier on the promise of free cocaine and drinks. On and on he goes about his new batch of cocaine's purity, catching Glesni, the more conventionally pretty of two's attention more than Delyth's, who's at her first party of the sort having been led astray from her strict, well-behaved upbringing by Glesni. Both started off their drug-taking in the previous months, taking MDMA two to three times a week, which is how they met Byron and grew curious of the wonders of other drugs out there. Delyth's attention fixates on the sheer delight glittering on Damo's face as he pours his first glass of gin. Noticing this, he smirks and pours three other shots.

Catching a glimpse of the trolley in his eye, Konrad cuts himself off mid-sentence, squares over and picks up the packet of burgers. "The one thing I asked of you." He holds up the split packet.

"Ah I'm so sorry mate, nightmare of a journey," Frankie fearfully blubbers.

Konrad shakes his head, pops two ten milligram Valium's from a fresh strip in his mouth, cracks open a stumpy beer with his teeth and washes them down with it. "All you're good for is your fucking gaff." He throws the Valium strip over to Frankie deliberately inaccurately and turns away to bag up a quarter ounce of weed.

Frankie scrambles to pick it up off the greasy floor near Damo and Byron's feet. To his horror, he spots two missing and runs over to confront Konrad. "One strip a week, all I ask for." Konrad callously ignores Frankie, not even turning to face him. "I don't give you no shit, I keep to myself, I don't whinge when I can't go no kip."

Ali and Derfel storm in energetically, cutting Frankie off in his tracks, both holding two carrier bags each stuffed with 660ml bottles of Kronenberg.

"You wanted a dirty sesh." Derfel shakes up a bottle, chips the kitchen surface while cracking it open with it and sprays it around the room. Part of it lands on Damo and

168

Byron who take it in good spirits, but most of it's on Frankie and Dolly, who don't share the same zest for his actions. "Well you've fucking got one."

Konrad glances back at Frankie with a subtle smirk and struts jovially over to Derfel and Ali. "Dinglers!" He claps hands with both.

Konrad hands Derfel the newly bagged quarter ounce and he takes it away mirthfully to a nearby surface, euphorically examining it, taking a deep whiff of inside the bag.

"Girl Scout cookies, man!" Derfel proudly shows Ali, who shrugs neutrally and tears a bit off one of the buds to make a joint. "Get yourself a whiff of that." Derfel sticks the bag in Frankie's face in an attempt to garner the positive reaction he so desperately desires. Frankie sniffs it and nods unconvincingly, not seeing anything special in the stuff. "Brama or wha'?" Having given up on his quest, Derfel throws some tobacco into a king skin.

"How's the diet going, mate?" Frankie tentatively asks.

Derfel throws the tobacco down and bullishly gets in Frankie's face. "What you on about diet you gimpy little fuck!" He rips the strip of Valium out of Frankie's hand, stuffs one in his mouth and holds them up. "Vallys are my diet mate. So I'll have them all day."

Frankie reaches for the strip, but using his gangly height, Derfel maneuvers them out of his reach. Frankie's attempts at snatching them becomes progressively tenacious, to the amusement of all in the room bar Glesni and Delyth, who look on in sympathy.

"Let the lad have his dear jellies," Konrad says through hysterical laughter.

"No fucking way!" Derfel insists.

"He won't stop crying. Let him have them." Konrad throws Derfel two full strips of strong thirty milligram Valium's.

Moderately satisfied with the compromise, Derfel chucks Frankie's strip out of the window and into a shallow puddle in the yard. Frankie darts outside to get them, becoming drenched by thundering rain and runs upstairs, guarding his dear soggy strip of Valium close to his chest. He chucks three in his mouth, a heavier dose than usual, and turns up Match of the Day on his screechy old telly to maximum volume, only partially blocking out the monsoon of noise from downstairs.

For Delyth's first time at a party such as this, she's got the hang of sniffing lines down to a tee. Despite the near enough certainty of being ostracized by her local politician and staunchly anti-drug father should he find out, she feels at home. Never more so than after sniffing her sixth deliberately chunky line made up by Dolly – with the last one having had a bit of speed thrown in on the sly.

"Swift little learner you," Dolly proudly says.

This line understandably hits Delyth differently. She fidgets and struggles to sit still. Her head twitches erratically towards the kitchen and back, her breathing becomes noticeably heavier.

"Never felt less judged, my whole life," Delyth intensely tells Dolly with a mammoth gurn as she passes over the plate.

"What happens when you find the right people." Dolly dips her head down to take a line and turns to Delyth before doing so. "Spiritual alignment." She devours the line.

Over in the kitchen, Damo and Ali watch on as Derfel acts out fighting scenarios.

"What you do aye." Derfel pretends to jab a finger in each of Ali's eyes. Catching him off guard, he flinches backwards. "Fucking straight in for the googles like that." Derfel takes advantage of Ali's disorientation by swivelling around and locking his arms under Ali's shoulders from behind. Ali fiercely tries to escape to no avail.

Damo pitifully scoffs and pulls four red boxing gloves out of the kitchen cupboard. "I'll ref." He holds the gloves out to Derfel and Ali.

"Fuck am I sparring loony the first man," Ali fearfully says, with the concussion suffered after he was stupid enough to last New Year's Eve still ringing in his ears.

Derfel rips the gloves out of Damo's hand, puts them on and adopts a gangly southpaw boxing stance. "I'll spark you both out two on one, guaranteed." Damo and Ali look at each other, Ali shakes his head. Derfel gets down on his knees. "You lot don't even have to wear gloves. Give me the chance Al!"

"Not on that one bit," Ali says.

"Fucking pea head." Derfel gets up in a huff.

"I'll spar vegan here, though." Ali points at Damo, who nods.

"No one ever spars me man!" Derfel slams the gloves down on the floor, chugs a beer and rolls a joint within their makeshift boxing ring. "Not moving."

Ali grins and throws the gloves on, Damo sets a three minute timer on the microwave and throws on the other pair.

Over on the sofa, Byron holds a plate with a chunky line and a mini mountain of a gram's worth of cocaine to Glesni, with whom he's been been trying desperately, without reciprocation, to chat up all night. She swiftly vacuums it up with a note, rubbing her nose hard afterwards.

"Absolute natural with the five bar note I see," Byron says with seductive sleaze.

"One of my many talents," Glesni cuttingly responds while racking up another line from the pile.

"You know, it's just nice to have birds round here for once. Not many have the guzzler for this sordid sack of a hell hole," Byron says.

Derfel squeezes himself in between Byron and Glesni, pushes Byron off the sofa and snogs Glesni without invitation. Although met with shock initially, she quickly reciprocates. Byron watches in bewilderment before scuttling off to watch the boxing unfold in the kitchen. Ali throws a sharp jab and body combination at Damo, whose slick head movement manoeuvres him around most of them. His hands boldly kept down offering no head protection, with the ones landing only glancing his face. Damo comes back at him with a right cross, landing flush on Ali's jaw as he leans in. Despite a loud crack, the punch fails to move Ali's head whatsoever. He swivels his neck back and devilishly smiles, ready for more. Byron cheers.

After a mere minute and a half of foreplay, Derfel leads Glesni out of the room by her hand and up the stairs into the houses now famous 'shagging room'. Unluckily for Frankie, this is the room directly next to his. It being designated in this way makes no logical sense, given Guy's far bigger room with an actual bed instead of bending the girls, or guys in Damo's occasional case, over a chest of draws or doing it on the wall. Derfel elects for the wall this time, as poor Frankie lies on his bed miserably watching a B horror movie on Film 4, unwittingly lapping up every second of Glesni's

173

muzzled theatrical moaning. As Frankie necks two more Valium out of the strip and necks them down with a beer. A loud slam of Konrad's customers barging in through the front door alarms him, causing him to cough on the beer and Valium partly lodged in his throat. But he recovers quickly enough to regain his breath. Glesni ferociously orgasms, which brings an end to at least one of the sources of irritating noises firing Frankie close to a sensory overload.

"Glad you didn't fuck Wee wee now aren't you?" Derfel says, quickly snorting two quick fire keys of cocaine one after another. "Bit of that?"

"Not that bash garb that's flying round down there no?" Glesni asks.

"I'll fucking have it then," Derfel says after a pause, thoroughly offended by Glesni's lack of gratitude.

Derfel loudly guzzles another two keys worth of coke before his thudding footsteps head towards Frankie's door, he smashes into it repeatedly. "Slashing out the window if you don't let me in!" He shouts. A heavy box with two five kilo dumbbells used to block the door is blown away. Derfel barges in bollock naked with his trousers around his ankles. "This ain't the bog no?"

Alfie suffered viscerally following his self-inflicted local humiliation, with insult to injury added through his one-hundred-hour community service sentence, served stacking the local British Heart Foundation's charity shop shelves. One of the only things that made it better was that he only had to stack the bottom shelves he could reach from a sitting position. A broken leg from the crash, which he's still in a cast for now, meant he couldn't stand up. Taking pity on him, the manager often chalked off five hours at a time despite him only doing one. Such was the humiliation, he's not dared show his face at any of the local snooker clubs where he remains a laughingstock for having lied so publicly about turning pro, essentially confirming his retirement from the game. His cushty life at home with his parents, not having to pay rent, was brought to an end that day as well. Not for the arrest and community order, but for the shame they felt due to his lies and the ridiculing behind his father Harry's back at the boisterous factory where he works as a line manager. As such, Alfie's had to make do with a surprisingly expensive rundown studio flat that swallows his entire income.

Never has the nosedive Alfie *'One Visit'* Fenner's life took from the heights of being on the verge of securing a place on the snooker pro tour been more evident than on this particularly grotty night. Down in the dimly lit Peep nightclub's toilet, his unspectacular display of lotions, aftershaves, deodorants and towels sits behind him. Having been a particularly poor night of takings, he leans against the display with his pink and black snooker gilet on, as it has been practically everywhere since his fateful day attempting to secure the big time. Sean, a regular in the club who comes in by himself to pull women, most of the time unsuccessfully, lies passed out on the floor in a recovery position that Alfie put him in ten minutes earlier. Done out of pity and in order to shield him from the bouncers, who'd have gladly lobbed him out the door hours ago.

Guto and Bryn stumble out of the same toilet cubicle sneezing, both almost identical in looks with shaved sides and the same tracksuit bottoms. All that separates them is Bryn's slightly darker shade of maroon red Moncler polo shirt in comparison to Guto's. Both having spent twenty minutes in there getting as coked up as possible before heading home to their equally strict parents before seeing out the night listening to dub techno on headphones until the buzz wears off.

"Take it easy boys," Alfie says.

Guto flings water out of his palm into Alfie's face, sending Bryn into hysterics. "In a bit mate," he sarcastically says, imitating a Cornish accent.

Alfie firmly wipes the water off his face. Seething inside, but without the courage to say anything, he sits down and lights a fag. Sean groans on the floor, a perfect opportunity to take his bitterness out on him.

"Get up!" Alfie prods Sean with his crutch, sapping enough of a reaction from him to just about lift his head up and rest his chin on the urinal edge, which he projectile vomits into. "Lightweight dick."

That's it, all of his display is shoved brashly into his black holdall an hour early, he's had it. Three months off the coke are over, tonight is the night. His only issue being deciding on how much is enough, a decision quickly rounded up to an eighth, leaving a cheeky few bumps' worth possibly left over to face the bogs tomorrow and fuel the courage to tell Guto where to stick it.

Freshly stung by Glesni's rejection, Byron wipes butane hash oil on a king size rizla in the middle of a credit card shaped pipe, intent on getting as stoned as possible. His razor-sharp focus is marred by his phone ringing. Alfie's calling, it shows up on his screen as *'Hollywood One Visit'*, as he's commonly referred to by swathes of the community as of late. He chuckles and answers the call.

"The lad of all lads, Alfie One Visit Fenner, how the fuck is Hollywood?" Byron mockingly asks.

"Scrubbing away as per," Alfie drearily remarks.

"Are you yeah? Last I heard you'd hit the big time."

"All have our ups and downs boy," Alfie nervously responds.

"Sure it wasn't your fault mate," Byron lethargically says, ruing the decision to ever ask. He tears up a Marlboro gold fag and crumbles the tobacco onto the table.

"Any chance of an eight ball on tick mate?"

"Look I don't know you, do I?"

"Didn't say that."

"Yeah, so why would I start you off with a three-and-a-half-gram tick?"

"Course not, you're spot on, shouldn't have asked, sure I can sort something out, sorry for asking." Alfie trips over his words.

Byron nods sarcastically. "Nah, nah, don't worry about it at all. Swing by tonight, come have a jar!"

"Be right there mate."

"Sound, but it's five hundred this time." Byron tears roach off a rizla packet.

"Shit the bed Wee wee."

"Well for the A grade in stock, that's a no brainer lad."

"All right, all right."

"Sound, in a bit, in a bit, yeah." Byron pulls the phone away, relieved at having finished the call. Looking forward to his largest sale of the day, he tucks his black oil covered rizla and lights the tingling spliff.

"All right then Wee wee, five hundred for an eight ball," Damo says in astonishment.

"It's that snooker prick. Absolute gimp of a bloke, hundred, just to get through that door," Byron assertively belts out.

"Spends decent money though don't he?" Konrad disapprovingly says without looking up, fearful Byron's tarnished any hope of repeat business.

"He wants to bang on about being some big shot snooker cunt, when he works down in a filthy bog, shotting rare bear knock off aftershave, then he can pay top whack. And the fucking rest," Byron insists.

Konrad turns away, thoroughly put in his place for once in his domineering life. His irritation is short lived as he claps eyes on Dolly initiating Delyth into the crack cocaine world, leaving a great chance of Konrad having gained an extra customer, although her utter uselessness with a lighter proves a stumbling block initially. Dolly impatiently grabs the lighter and lights the horizontal shaped pipe held to Delyth's mouth with her first attempt. She rips a hefty toke on it, grimaces but carries on like a trooper.

"Don't you dare stop. Will not be happy if you waste any," Dolly fiercely claims.

Konrad gazes on eagerly and winks at Dolly. She smirks back, knowing a finder's fee of at least the wiping off of a score from her debt is on the cards. Delyth's eyes flutter as she pulls the pipe away from her lip. She lays back on the sofa, her head twitches towards the kitchen periodically.

After half an hour of Byron pranging for Alfie's arrival, determined to withhold getting fully spangled until after his business for the day is done, his moment arrives. He lets

Alfie in, powering ahead without patience to wait for him to hobble down the corridor and waves his arms out theatrically to present Alfie to the room as he enters.

"One visit lad, how's it going?" Damo says with inauthentic warmth. He rushes over and carefully takes off his chunky bag. "Will fit into our cloak room impeccably I'd have thought."

Damo swiftly returns and pours the pair hefty pink gin servings. They tap their shot glasses together and chug them simultaneously.

"Sweet as mate. Devine that is." Alfie wrings out his face out and snorts a key of cocaine.

"None of these shit shows would be seen dead drinking it." Damo pours another two shots.

"Yeah, I'd rather you didn't tell any of the snooker lads about it and all." Alfie holds a key brimming with cocaine near Damo's nose that's swiftly dealt with.

Damo taps his glass against Alfie's and they neck down their shots, with Damo reacting the stronger of the two on this occasion. "Who's your er, main practice squeeze these days then? Still Dom Dale?"

"Nah, sacked that peasant off donkeys ago boy. Squirm didn't have it in him," Alfie boldly claims, not realizing that everyone in the town is aware of his retirement.

Damo struggles to restrain a chuckle and turns away to avoid detection, then pours another two shots from the now half empty bottle.

"Rick Walden these days really. He just about competes."

Alfie looks around the room. "What about old Frank boy, where's he at? Handy ain't he?"

"Oh, proper character round the gaff he is. Yeah, I do like Frankie."

"Do you?"

"Hell of a lot actually."

Alfie tokes on his fag and stares Damo in the eye. "Flaky cunt will let you down one day bert. Grasped that the hard way."

"Top soldier is Frankie." Damo turns away to pour another shot but turns back before pouring it. "Think I have a chance?

"A chance?"

"You know, what are my chances?" Damo bluntly asks.

Alfie's eyebrows lift up, initially surprised at the mere concept of Frankie being gay, he ponders before nodding. "Got a few zans, bit of bugle on you. More than a chance with him these days mate."

Damo cups his mouth, mimicking concern. "You think! Tragic what a state it is some people get in."

"Any sympathy for that dweeb I had shattered the day he got his old man sent down. What kind of horrible cunt does that? Not as if Gibbo killed him did he? Prick deserves everything he gets, snaky little thing. Guy's life's fucked."

Damo swigs out of the pink gin bottle while staring at Alfie. "Like your style."

Derfel bursts into the room topless, singing the lyrics to 'Dani California - Red Hot Chilli Peppers'. Glesni follows shortly after and scurries into the living room, uncomfortable with the beady attention on her as she enters.

"Quite the natter." Damo winks at Alfie, struts over to Derfel with the pink gin in hand, and sings wildly to 'Dani California'. Derfel grabs the bottle off Damo and swigs some without his lips touching the bottle, spilling some on his chest. He spits it out and pours some on his head.

Derfel bursts into Frankie's room, obliterating the makeshift door stop and chipping the bottom corner of the door frame. Frankie's just finishing a piss in his sink, he rushes to pull his trousers up and cowers on his bed.

"Will you just fuck off Derfel!" Frankie hysterically shouts.

Derfel walks over to the back of the bed. "Wish it were that simple. This is a socio-political matter that just can't be swerved." He forcibly grabs Frankie's hands and handcuffs them to the bed frame. "Drastic action's the only way."

Frankie wildly flaps his legs as Damo enters holding a roll of thick masking tape. "Not enough having the whole house for your gain, got to fuck with me and all have you?"

182

Damo and Derfel hold Frankie's legs and tape them together. He fears nothing overly sinister, as he's been subject to a plethora of similar pranks in the recent past.

"You're just too much competition for the birds downstairs lad." Derfel says with a grin.

"I don't fucking like any of your birds," Frankie insists.

"Far from the issue in hand," Derfel says.

"Swear down," Frankie pleads.

"It's you they're after I'm afraid, and numbers are shaky as it is," Derfel pedantically claims, leaning in to Frankie's face.

"And as per your exemplary co-operation in helping us create a fair and safe environment for all to flourish in." Damo takes three Valium out of a strip and dangles them in front of Frankie with an unnerving smirk.

"Nah, nah. I'm already off my chops," Frankie desperately utters.

Damo drops all three pills in Frankie's mouth, he struggles to swallow them and gasps for air. Damo holds his nose and pours half a can of Carling down his throat.

"The fuck." Derfel shudders and turns pale, finding this sadistic even by his standards.

Damo eventually lets go of Frankie's nose and he gasps harrowingly for air. After allowing him to take in a good few breaths, Damo tapes up his mouth. "Now you're gonna' be here until the birds leave, ok mate? Hope that's all right yeah."

Damo grabs the TV remote and sticks on a Freeview porn channel, one with a naked lady prancing around that can only be heard audibly through paying eighty pence a minute. He nods his head towards the door, gesturing for him and Derfel to leave. Derfel takes a guilty look back at Frankie, who's surprisingly calm given the circumstances and briskly walks out. They head downstairs to find everyone but Alfie chaotically raving to a roller's drum and bass tune, the party having well and truly kicked off.

"See ya' in a bit boy," Alfie tells Byron. With barely a hint of a response, he unassertively hobbles his way through the crowd and walks out.

'Big Al – Steps (In Deep we Trust Mix)' blares out of the speaker and is met by a collective roar of enthrallment. Konrad and Ali snort chunky lines and everyone goes mad for the tune. Derfel joins in far less enthusiastically than the rest.

After what feels like a ten-hour doze, but is more like two, Frankie wakes up lying towards the door to his pants being pulled down from behind. He screams, his mouth cover muffles the sound and he thrusts his legs at the assailant, which shimmy's him over to be lying flat on his back. Spotting it's Damo, he walks over to face him, grinning evilly, sweating buckets with his eyes bulging.

"Flapping's only gonna' make it worse," Damo sadistically claims in a sing song manner.

Frankie weeps and flails every body part available to him as much as his restrictions allow.

Growing frustrated by Frankie's lack of submission, Damo grabs hold of him. "Fuck this."

Damo lets go and smacks Frankie on the jaw with two consecutive downward hard hooks that daze Frankie and slow him down. Unsatisfied by the results, Damo shakes his head and lands another punch to Frankie's midriff. Frankie whimpers as blood trickles from a cut under his eye. Damo takes a four-inch skin coloured dildo out of his pocket.

"Just gonna' loosen you up a bit." Damo throws Frankie over to face the door and rubs his chest.

Frankie screams as Damo quickly thrusts the dildo up his arse. This goes on for a couple of minutes, with Frankie becoming mute after the first few. Damo then gets out his kit and masturbates violently, only taking twenty seconds to climax. He pulls up his trousers and heads towards the door, biting his lip, nodding and appearing thoroughly proud of himself.

"Now I'm just getting to know you at this point, not really sure where you've been, so, be difficult for me to say, when I'm ready to take the plunge, move this forward a bit. But you're doing everything right so far," Damo adds, leaving Frankie sprawled out on the bed.

185

A few hours later, during which time Damo came up and unlocked the handcuffs, Frankie wakes up to Dolly shouting in his dried blood-covered face. He slowly gains consciousness as Dolly peels the tape off his mouth, only managing to do so partly before Frankie backs away.

"Get away. Get away now!" Frankie slurs, the Valium still affecting his senses and ability to speak coherently all these hours later.

Suddenly, he realizes his hands are free and scrambles to rip off the tape, first from his mouth and then his legs. Dolly reaches over tentatively to help him. Frankie backs off and holds his clenched fist up.

"Get your fucking hands off me!" Frankie warns as he bulldozers past her, knocking her to the floor. Without his phone, or any belongings but the clothes on his back, he limps down the stairs and stumbles out of the door.

After reaching the town centre five minutes away, it dawns on him that he brought nothing along, including his tobacco. Beginning to feel dizzy and becoming increasingly disorientated, he's drawing peculiar looks from pedestrians, some worried for him, with others finding his plight hilarious, including a group of four young chav teenagers. Nobody steps in, with most assuming him to just be a heroin addict, including a mother with four kids who warns them not to stare. Frankie approaches a mousey, frail looking pedestrian in a cheap dark suit.

"Can I borrow your phone?" Frankie asks with a hoarse voice.

"Out of credit mate." The pedestrian fearfully backs away and speeds off in the opposite direction.

Frankie sticks his swollen head into his hands, which get covered in fresh blood stemming from his nose. He stumbles over to the open window of Clio Lounge restaurant and falls into the vacant window ledge, bouncing out onto the concrete via cracking his chest on an empty plastic table. On this occasion, people do scurry over to help in droves, ironically after it's too late.

Having been quoted a three hour wait for an ambulance, a community police officer takes him up to hospital in their cop car. Frankie's rectum leaks out blood on route, staining the seats and leaving the officer secretly bewailing the decision to take him up, dreading the potential added hour of his shift to clean it up.

They decide to keep him in overnight, to be assessed by a mental health team tomorrow. His retina is detached again however, the same one previously damaged, and he's sustained nasty internal bruising around his rectum such was the force used by Damo. After being left alone for a couple of hours, Dyfrig, a suave detective in his fifties with

187

tidy hair in a brown leather jacket cautiously enters Frankie's cubicle, his jacket beaming under the hospital's bright lights. Closely behind him is his stern partner Ioan, whose shaved buzz cut only adds to his unsavoury aura, not someone you'd want to meet in a dark alley.

"You're not in trouble okay Frankie?" Dyfrig softly says. Frankie barely lifts his head up in acknowledgment. "I'm Detective Sergeant Dyfrig Rowlands."

"And I'm Detective Constable Ioan Ellis," Ioan adds.

"You're not obliged to speak to us in any way. We know you had absolutely bugger all to do with the–" Dyfrig ponders. "Alleged operations, commencing at your address. We just want to help punish who did this to you."

"One of the trap house lads was it?" Ioan abrasively asks. Dyfrig glares at Ioan.

Frankie lightly nods. "Damo." He quickly says, barely having to think about the pros and cons of revealing his identity.

Ioan and Dyfrig gaze at each other with grave concern.

"Are you referring to Damien Hayward?" Ioan says his name carefully.

Both are already highly familiar with Damo. Ioan in particular, having found out he'd been texting his fourteen-year-old daughter, a fortunate discovery before their planned meet went ahead. Although due to Damo making the texts non sexual, no charges prevailed for that incident.

188

Frankie nods and collapses into the bed, tears streaming down his face. "Him and a, a bunch of his goons. They moved into my house. Took it over. Was only supposed to be him and Byron Wee wee, for a few days. Didn't pan out like that. Had their boss, fat fucking Konrad living there, horrible cunt. People in and out for ket, vallys, scag the fucking lot!" He has a break and takes deep breaths until he regains somewhat of his composure. "Look, I could just about cope with all that, get on with my day. I mean, I didn't have a fucking choice. But Damo." His voice evaporates as he struggles to get his words out.

"Take all the time you need boi," Ioan reassures Frankie.

"It started off just, him coping a feel and that once in a while, you know, when I walked by or whatever."

Frankie goes on to tell them every last detail of the horrendous event and everything that preceded it. Both Ioan and Dyfrig leave shocked to the core, which especially for Ioan takes some doing. Never has a case been as important as this one in their careers.

Glesni, Derfel, Ali and Delyth lie asleep on uncomfortable makeshift beds in the designated shagging room with thin blankets. Glesni's spooning Derfel, while Ali and Delyth face one another with their hands around each other. Derfel jumps up and overcome by paranoia, he looks out the

189

window to see a black Mercedes parked outside, with a Police van pulling up and another one behind it.

"Shit the bed man!" Derfel sprints over to Ali and shakes him. "Al! Get up now!"

With no luck getting a response, Derfel shoves two sealed bags with seven grams of cocaine into his pocket and slaps Ali on the back of the head, still no response. Ali's body has been entirely depleted after sniffing at least four grams of bash the night before.

Glesni and Delyth wake up among the commotion, Delyth peeks out of the window and frantically throws on her clothes. "Gwell bo' nhw m'yn deutha ffocin dad fi de cont."

"Tyd flaen a neutha nhw ddim," Derfel ferociously tells her. "Al! Get your Kenny, now! Cops are gonna' be flying in here any second."

Ali stretches his arm out to push Derfel away but misses. "I'm shagging mate," he mumbles, still half asleep.

Derfel slaps Ali on the forehead again, this time with the desired effect. "NWP are coming for your gear, you dingler fuck!"

Ali's eyes burst open. He jumps up, scrambles to collect his half ounce bags of cocaine and ketamine and sloppily throws his stripy t-shirt on the wrong way around.

Derfel grabs two half-drunk beers off the side, throws a bag of ketamine over to Ali and walks out. "Not waiting for you."

All four run out of the room. With Ali still putting on his trousers, he lags behind. At the top of the stairs, Derfel sticks his finger on his mouth and chugs a beer as they all tiptoe down the stairs and sneak into the living room. Byron and Dolly lie sprawled out on a folded-out sofa bed, Byron spoons Dolly from a comically long distance away. Konrad and Damo both lie fast asleep, sat upright on the other sofa with Damo's snoring mouth being wide open. Derfel lobs his empty beer bottle at the wall, that with the cutting loud knocks from the front door wake Konrad, Damo, Dolly and Byron up.

"Raid of the century outside boys," Derfel warns them before sprinting out, followed by the others.

"All the best," Ali says to Konrad.

Appearing by far the most anxious, Damo peeks out of the window. He shuts them in horror and crouches down out of sight. Having been in this situation on numerous occasions, Konrad urgently grabs three bags of disposable wipes and gets to work. First scrubbing off the residue covering trays and cases, then throwing all the smaller bags of cocaine down the sinkhole.

"I'm done for here." Damo punches the table full pelt.

"Fucking shut up man! Get rid of all the residue, little bits and we're sound." Konrad pelts a bag of wipes at Byron, who's not possessing quite the level of urgency needed as he gathers his senses. "And you and all Wee wee!"

Byron belatedly gets going with wiping down the table and dropping his personal stash of ketamine down the sink.

"Cheers for the glorious opportunities you've afforded me Keez," Damo blubbers.

Konrad suspiciously gazes over at Dolly and Byron, who are both blank. Sensing there's something he's missing, he glares back at Damo sternly. "They're not gonna' find the big bits, not where I've stashed them. Be fucking sure of that."

Konrad's interrupted by the bashing open of the front door. He claps his ears, grimaces and closes his eyes while enduring a flashback of a similar memory at the age of nine. Two kitted-up riot officers march upstairs shouting, 'Police! This is a raid!' repeatedly and tear apart the bedroom, chucking everything left off the shelves around. Another two head into the living room. Dyfrig and Ioan waltz in, cool, calm, collected and full of hope. Damo's face sinks to new lows, knowing exactly who Ioan is and the problems he will no doubt impose.

"I'm Detective Sergeant Dyfrig Rowlands and this is Detective Constable Ioan Ellis. Doubt I really need to bore you with what's happening here."

Riot officers aggressively investigate the kitchen area while Dyfrig goes over the formalities.

"North Wales Police special, tearing apart another perfectly civilized household, for fuck all! That's what's happening," Konrad responds.

Dyfrig sarcastically nods at Ioan. "That civilized, that we just left sniffers in the car. For their own safety."

"Bastards! Not only do you take those dogs lives away, their freedom, to be your little slaves. But then you bring them places when you don't even need them! Cruel as they come, unforgivable misuse of us taxpayers' dough," Dolly berates the sniggering officers. "The lot of this is."

"Don't you worry Dollington, they'll make a cameo if required." Ioan boots a bit of stray broken glass off the floor that hits Damo on the shoulder. "Just clearing up first."

Damo doesn't dare react and keeps his quivering gaze well away from Ioan. Konrad gets up and puffs out his chest.

"Pipe down you meatball cunt. I'll flatten you," Ioan warns Konrad.

A riot officer clatters his heavy feet down the stairs and hands Dyfrig a plastic sealed bag with Damo's dildo inside. "Amateur hour." He adds before rushing back upstairs.

"It's not mine!" Damo blurts out, feeling the wrath of Dyfrig and Ioan's piercing glares.

"Problem we have is that it matches the description of the very object used to carry out a seedy sexual assault--" Dyfrig says with his eyes fixated on Damo.

"To put it mildly," Ioan chimes in.

"At this very address, this very morning," Dyfrig adds with a sarcastically confused tone.

Konrad grits his teeth and glares at Damo. "Fucked up you have lad!"

"Come with us will you, we can rule you out! And find out whose this really is," Ioan tells Damo.

Dyfrig bends down to face Damo. "Wouldn't even be here if it were just the gear." He says while looking at Konrad at the same time. "Damien Hayward, you are under arrest on the suspicion of sexual assault by penetration and possession with the intent to supply class A drugs." He roughly throws the handcuffs on Damo. Konrad spits on the floor.

"Dandruff isn't a class A anymore mate," Dolly points out.

"Yeah, how can you do him for A's?" Byron adds.

Dyfrig and Ioan head towards the sofa. "Up!" Ioan shouts at Konrad, who doesn't budge. "You were warned lard arse." Ioan picks Konrad up by the shoulders and launches him into the kitchen, sending him stumbling into Damo. Konrad shoves him violently into the wall to cushion his fall.

Dyfrig uncompromisingly rips off the sofa cushions, sticks his hand deep under into the crevices and proudly presents a loose gram sized bud of weed. "Bit of that ground up on the steak and chips after!" He gratefully pockets it.

Ioan bends down onto the floor and pulls out a quarter ounce bag of ketamine from the tight gap under the sofa. Byron's vacant expression turns into one of despair.

"Should just about do it for now!" Dyfrig boasts.

"That's ketamine actually lads," Dolly snarkily points out.

Ioan pulls a sarcastically fearful face at Dyfrig. "Only a b Dyf! Forgot ket was legal?"

"We might as well just fuck off now!" Dyfrig mockingly adds, interrupted by a snarling bark from a couple of dogs scuttling up the stairs. He grins at Ioan victoriously.

All are cuffed and taken by riot officers towards the van with little fuss made, all having resigned themselves to their immediate fate. This can't be said for Damo, who's taken away kicking and screaming separately to the Mercedes with Ioan and Dyfrig.

"I want to go in the van with them," Damo begs, fearing their suspicions that he may be grassing if taken in separately.

"New 'no rapist' policy on the van mate," Dyfrig fiercely whispers in his ear.

Ioan swivels Damo around to face Konrad, Byron and Dolly as they're loaded onto the police van. "Say bye bye to the lads." He holds Damo's arm and mimics a floppy wave with it before slamming him head first into the car, so hard that he's lodged into the gap between seats.

That's not where the day's brutality ends for Damo. After his no comment interview, they leave him in the dark room for half an hour. With the promise of a blind eye being turned, they return with Gavin to batter the sexual deviant to within the brink of consciousness. Only stopping when Ioan brings in a pole and threatens to shove it up Damo's arse, a point when Gavin and Dyfrig realize enough is enough. They leave him in Gavin's capable hands whose night shift it is that evening in the holding cells. Relishing this opportunity down to his respect for Frankie, he launches Damo into the cell once everyone's done with him. Damo clatters into the wall head first and collapses onto the bed, crying his eyes out, with his face cut around his eyes and blood spewing out of his mouth. He attempts to sit up against the wall with great difficulty and coughs up blood as the door slams shut.

Chapter 9 - In the drink

Delyth's father had grown tired of her lies a *long* time before the fateful night of the raid, and had long suspected her of drug use, way before it was ever a problem, given his tendency to think the worst of the family's scapegoat. His connections with people high up in the policing service through his political work ensured he found out the minute Byron and Damo got taken in. As such, following a furious forty-eight hours of rampant sex and sniffing speed with Derfel, Ali, and Glesni in Ali's grotty halfway house bedroom, she stumbled home. Shivering from the cold sweat of her horrific comedown, only to disastrously find her essentials sprawled out in bin bags outside their four-bedroom detached Garth family house.

With little choice in the matter, she sought Dolly out, who'd been the only one released without charge. Reluctantly, Dolly let her crash on the floor of her council owned studio flat. What was initially hoped to be a week turned into a month, with both enjoying each other's company despite the cramped surroundings. Other than having to leave the flat when Dolly got the occasional in call from a bloke on AdultWork – something that her poor rating on the site meant was becoming increasingly infrequent –

this worked out for Delyth. She'd longed for this type of closeness and supposed understanding for a long time. What this did mean was that her drug use sky rocketed. Such was her abuse of crack, that she was tempted into trying heroin a few weeks later by Dolly, on the promise it would help the unbearable come downs. Part of Dolly's willingness to accommodate her stemmed from the two grand in savings Delyth had accumulated that summer working in the Snowdon Mountaintop Cafe – only saved up because of her then-sobriety. But as this inevitably dwindled, along with Dolly's income, tensions between the two began to intensify, and after a month they both now spend their daytimes begging on Bangor high street in-between Dolly's occasional paid romp.

On one of these dreary days, the rainiest of the winter so far, Delyth spends the early morning tearing down every one of her father's campaign posters. Titled 'Rheinallt Parry MP – Plaid Cymru' and with a headshot of his speckled, gawky face looking righteous and wearing an ill-fitting suit, she's doing Bangor a favour. Her motivations being to stifle his campaign to retain the Arfon seat in the upcoming general election. Proud of her morning's work, she struts over to Dolly who's sitting miserably under the doorway of a derelict old shop, a dusty sleeping bag over her as most pass by barely looking her way. Spotting a kind looking young man cruising past on a longboard, Dolly jumps up.

"Excuse me there gent, spare a lass a squiddy would you?" She confidently asks.

Apologetically, he throws two Benson and Hedges fags and ten pence into the pouch set out for collecting change. "All I've got sorry." He holds a peace sign up with his fingers as he cruises off. "Blessed."

Dolly blows him a kiss and lights one of the fags up. After no time, she spots another potential target, a short, suited passer-by. "Couldn't spare two down-and-outters some scrilla could you please fine sir?" She puts on a vulnerable tone.

"Might as well jam a prick up your vein myself," he boldly responds in a posh Kent accent.

"Matey here needs bus fare, final round of chemo actually!" Dolly shouts as the suited man speeds off.

After a few miserable unprofitable hours, and with the thundering rain forming puddles verging on reaching the slightly elevated level of their empty shop door, a ping on Dolly's phone delights her. She shows Delyth the confirmation of a double female order, or FF as the site abbreviates it.

"FF. The fuck. You mean?" Delyth folds her arms. Dolly nods with a wry smile. "Never said nothing about that."

"Oh come on. We've got to now," Dolly forcefully insists.

"Cunt you are," Delyth nods, not needing much time to think.

Dolly jumps up, dances over to her sleeping bag and stuffs it in a mountaineering rucksack.

"I won't fucking touch you. Even if he begs." Dolly gets in Delyth's face, her eyes manically bulge out. "Two hundred and forty bar mate. Sesh we're gonna' have after."

"Chucks another oner in the mix, then do with me as you so wish," Delyth energetically responds, buoyed by the choice of poison that will be available to her after this seedy deed.

They leg it off to the bus station's public toilets and lock themselves into separate grim cubicles with shit-stained toilets and overflowing needle bins on the wall. Dolly throws on her best makeup – saved for orders above eighty pounds – and changes into a blouse firmly revealing her C cup cleavage.

"Chuck us a cig Del," Dolly asks.

Yet to finish her makeup, Delyth lobs a fag into Dolly's cubicle and it lands straight in the filthy toilet water. "In the fucking drink, you absolute drip," Dolly barks. "Chucking another over or what?

Delyth grunts, annoyed at being interrupting midway through applying eye liner. She throws another over and drops the packet on the floor. In her attempt to bend down and pick it up, she knocks her hip into the needle bin and a few fall out without pricking her. After taking ten minutes to clear out all the dry dark blood from her nose with tissue, in which time two separate heroin addicts stand cuing for the cubicle to shoot up in, they're both prim and proper, ready to go. If they can get to Jewson's factory without the rain slithering off their makeup.

After a sombre day in the cells and having been warned he faces a minimum five-year sentence, it's fair to say Damo's mental state is hanging on a knife edge. Not least after the guarantee of being sent back to HMP Berwyn should he be sentenced, where not only will Konrad and Byron end up, but where he also owes a hundred pounds for cocaine. Not just to anyone, but the hardest cunt there, a vicious dealer that's still locked up – a debt he never paid after boldly thinking he'd never be sent back down to face it. However, after a Facebook message promising to 'Bum the living HIV into him' should he ever clap eyes on Damo again, he's well and truly bricking it for one of the first times in his adult life. Using the only means available to him, he decides to try and end it all. One by one he stuffs squares of tissue paper into his mouth, until about the fifth when he starts loudly gagging. Sat a mere two metres away from the cell and fresh from chugging three Monster energy drinks, Gavin beams a flashlight into the cell, storms in and snatches the bog roll off Damo, holding it up in front of him with his other hand holding Damo's floundering chin.

"Not leaving me that easily." Gavin sticks a blue disposable glove on, jams his finger down Damo's throat and holds his head over the bed until he vomits all over the thin bedding. Gavin repeats this then throws Damo's head down, leaving him in the cell alone in his own pool of bile.

Dolly and Delyth restlessly wait by the derelict Jewson's factory, furious with their customer pulling up half an hour after the agreed meeting time. Delyth trembles, not being as hardened to the cold as the hardy Dolly. Trudging slowly towards them in a brand-new saloon Mercedes with blank tinted windows is the grey haired, well-spoken Bangor golf club stalwart known only to prostitutes as 'Sir'. He lowers the window.

Dolly rests her arms on its ledge. "How are you Sir? Back for more I can't help but see."

"Certainly not from you, thieving little toe rag," Sir snaps back. He takes a look at Delyth, who's hovering a few metres away from the car smoking and sighs resentfully. "She'll have to do, by herself." Sir whistles Delyth over and turns to Dolly. "Bugger all like your profile. Joke shop."

Delyth sticks her head in the car window. "Half hour, fuck all more. And it's one fifty."

Sir rolls his eyes and eventually agrees. "We'll soon see if you're worth the hype." Delyth jumps into the back seat. Sir snaps his fingers and points to the front seat. "Front."

Delyth begrudgingly climbs through the middle of the front seats onto the passenger side. Sir panics as her muddy trainers muck up the motor's interior. Dolly's eye makeup trickles down her cheek as she watches them pulling off.

Upon return, Delyth's shaken up by her first ever paid rim job. It netted her an extra thirty-pound tip, that she will **not** be telling Dolly about. They head up the narrow Bangor Mountain path just in time for happy hour. Between six and seven, there's always a dealer waiting, being the only time of the day where an appointment isn't necessary, and therefore not followed by the inevitable extra twenty minutes of waiting. Good old reliable ginger Dave is duly there, dishing Richie a dressing down about the fifty pounds he owes for crack – an addiction that drastically spiraled, despite only having started taking cocaine in his thirties. He tells Richie to fuck off as he spots the girls heading up towards him. Richie subtly brushes past the both of them, catching a quick feel of their arses. This doesn't faze Dolly, but Delyth grimaces.

"Only doing ganj on the gram ladies," Dave asserts, having grown sick of Dolly trying her luck to reduce the prices of his quarter ounces.

"We'll have two brown, four white, and as many Vallys as thirty bar will bag us." Dolly cuts Delyth off before she can speak.

Dave's incredibly swift hands assemble the order in no time. He holds it out to Dolly, who glares at Delyth.

"I'll have, two brown, two white and a Q of green please," Delyth insists.

"As well?" Dave impatiently asks.

"If she's just shat a oner out of her arse, then yeah, both. But that's what I'm having." Delyth holds out eighty pounds.

"Fucking froogies man." Dave hastily puts some of the bags away.

"Comedown with no Vallys though!" Dolly vulnerably says, skint having spent the only three pounds she made from begging on a rare Tesco tuna and sweetcorn sandwich meal deal, her first proper meal in three days.

"Me that just rim jobbed that shrimpy fucking cretin, I'll get what I want." Delyth storms away up the mountain.

Dolly follows her in a huff while Dave enjoys the sight of their arses as they trudge off up to a filthy, shattered glass, empty beer can and nos canister ridden benched area overlooking Bangor University. Frankie's already waiting up there ready for them having clocked the two by Jewsons, knowing exactly where their predictable selves would end up after. He also feels owed after sharing his last batch of heroin with Dolly.

They kept in touch after the rape, mainly down to Frankie's newly spiraling heroin addiction, that gives Dolly a way to take something she needs from him. While he also conveniently allows her around to shoot up once in a while. He's sat on a graffiti drenched bench, swigging out of a one litre bottle of Jack Daniels. Dolly duly agrees to give him a hit, but one hit only, and not before she goes first, yanking the whiskey off of him for the first hefty swig of many in return. Delyth wraps a strap around Dolly's arm, holds the needle steady and injects her. Frankie watches on eagerly. With her work for the day done and determined to enjoy her own share after forking out for the entire feast of drugs, Delyth takes in a bustling pipes worth of crack. Dolly lies sprawled out on the bench passed out while Frankie wraps his arm with a strap, holding it in his mouth.

Two weeks into his five-year sentence, Damo's already repaid his one-hundred-pound debt with a series of sexual favours, including an evening of sucking off four of the dealers' associates. Not only because of this, his popularity is at an all-time low after loan made a point of telling all the prisoners about his liking for young girls. With Byron, Konrad and Derfel all now having been sentenced for their crimes and blanking him, a friendly smile by Brad, the lanky scouse kitchen head chef who's serving a ten-year sentence for credit card fraud, gives Damo butterflies.

Brad takes Damo's empty tray and grabs another one from underneath the counter that has sausage, mash and jelly on. "Christmas bonus for your graft lad."

"Cheers." Damo walks off suspiciously.

Damo spots Guy, Byron and Konrad on a table at the far end. None of them so much as peek his way. Not that he expected them to. So he heads over to a table where his cell mate Meirion, who was sentenced to six years for child porn offenses, sits alone. His hostile, hateful gaze leaves no question as to why. Damo subtly nods his head at him and doesn't get any more than a pitiful gaze in response. Damo plays around with his food, cuts off a small portion of sausage and winces as he chews it. Hard as rubber.

"Jelly, right upper corner. Side nearest to you," Meirion barks out without looking at Damo.

"Fuck are you having any of this," Damo declares.

"Jelly, right upper corner. Side nearest to you." Meirion militantly repeats without flinching or looking at Damo.

Damo grits his teeth. "Four days of hunger lad, going to have to be something pretty shit hot you want any of this."

Meirion impatiently sighs. "Have a look. Why on earth would I want that?"

Damo spots semen on his jelly, gags and pushes the tray away. "They forget to do all that now and then. When the spice is flying about." Meirion presents a bit fleghm from his plate on a chunk of uneaten turkey breast. "But those days. Few and fucking far between." Damo looks around the canteen and wearily sinks into his chair.

Hungry to the point of delirium, Damo lies on his cell bed pinching himself and tears little cuts into his arms.

Meirion forcefully applies face wash lotion, spots Damo struggling to even break his skin and scoffs. "Mate, all you've got to do." He snatches the nail clippers and cuts his nails into wonky, sharp shapes. "Bit sharp and wonky." He holds his hand up to Damo, who nods and tamely takes the clippers. Meirion returns his focus to the mirror and sniggers. "Going about that like the gimp you are."

Damo clips his finger nails into unorthodox shapes as demonstrated. Byron and Konrad sneak past the cell, which Meirion spots in the mirror. Damo rolls up his sleeves, ready to open up the half-arsed attempts at lacerations.

"Bit of classic Freeview on the big screen for me." Meirion walks backwards out of the room, adjusting his hair in view of the mirror until he gets to the doorway. "Meirion's the name and Jezza Kyle's my game."

Konrad subtlety nods at Guy as him and Byron pass by his cell, where he's reading FourFourTwo magazine on his bed. He grins, gets up, grabs an already boiled kettle, whacks a whole bag of sugar into the water and carefully folds the empty sugar packet into a plastic bag. After a bit of a stir, he marches into Damo's cell, kettle in hand and throws the content onto Damo's arms and chest.

"Be a lot lower than that next time boy," Guy warns before leaving him in the cell screeching in agony.

Guy rushes back to his cell, throws the kettle in the plastic bag and marches through the corridor. Many of the inmates, including Meirion, smile and nod in respect as he passes by, while others remain engrossed by the Jeremy Kyle repeat on telly. The very episode that got the show banned. A favourite of this group, that's watched at least weekly.

Already waiting by the shower door is Konrad while Guy strips down and hands over his clothes. Konrad hands Guy a fresh grey jumpsuit, stacks the incriminating clothes in a bag with the kettle and sugar packet, then urgently leaves straight out to the back. A pre-arranged delay of the dustbin lorry gives Konrad the chance to throw the bin bag on the back of it. He whistles, chucks his thumb up and the lorry drives off.

Guy scrubs himself down, a beaming sense of pride evident, as if all of his bad parenting was outdone in that one moment of clinical retribution. When in actual fact, he wouldn't have even considered doing it but for the added anger of Damo using his house for gay sex. That was the step too far for him, not the raping of his son. Konrad and Byron's debt and fear of him after using his place unbeknown, gives him every reason to believe the rest of this two-year sentence will be a dawdle.

Dazzler lies on his bed, dismayed at the lack of response from Frankie, who he sends the ninth unanswered text to in a period of six weeks. After having his transfer to Llangefni care home delayed due to a lack of space, it has been beating after beating for Dazzler. Without ever finding the right jui-jitsu move to get Ben down, he remains in fear of what might happen, with Wilder and Jonny having both been shipped out without him. Ben answers the front door after the doorbell's hammered for twenty seconds.

"Excuse me mate, sorry to bother you. Just we've had bare of your lads shotting next to our gaff," a scouse accented man at the door kindly relays.

Dazzler scrambles over to the window. A white- jacket-wearing scouser, one of Damo's dealer associates Jez, sporting a black shoulder length side fringed hairstyle is stood there.

"Have they now?" Ben says.

"Definitely green, but you never what else, that's all we can smell like. Didn't wanna' have to come here, but it's right where the little ones fuck about and that." Jez keeps word to word to the script he'll be paid forty pounds in cocaine for delivering that evening.

"Gone to police have you lad?" Ben asks after pondering momentarily.

"No, no, no, hoping to see how avoidable that was."

"Spot on. Won't happen again."

"Oh tah mate. Much appreciated." Jez slams the front door, throws his hood up, gets on his BMX and glares up viciously at Dazzler as he cycles off.

With no messing about, Ben comes thundering up the stairs. Dazzler closes his eyes, shaking and weeping, distraught that this cruel world's got the better of him. Ben smashes on the door; a draw blocks it. Dazzler grits his teeth, takes in some deep breaths and grabs a cloth from the side. Under the cloth lies a sharp shiny kitchen knife. Dazzler grips it with gusto, gathering his senses and composure, ready for battle.

THE END

WELSH TRANSLATIONS

Iesgo banol dad, be ti neud troma? - Jesus christ, what have you done now?

Dwin' iawn! - I'm Okay!

Su mai wa? - How's it going wa?

Bach – Small

Son am sanna chdi. - You were on about your socks

Mae'r hen foi de, wythdeg un wsos dwytha, a'r unig peth mae'n goro ddeud os mae o isho sex de 'di JULIA! Ma na ddigon yn capal yn barod amdani os dwi'm yn gal off y chdi, so tyd flaen neudi, fynu grisau na 'wan. - The old boy right, eighty one last week, and the only thing he's got to say when wants sex is JULIA! There's enough of them in chapel ready for it if I don't get it off you, so come on will you, up those stairs now.

Yli cont gwirion 'ma – Look at this stupid cont

Daliai cont! - Hold it cont!

Stoned gach yn gwaith eto. Ffocin nobed. Ffwc ti meddwl wti. Hamro vallys yn gwaith. Diawl o foi! - Stoned in work again. Fucking nob head. Fuck do you think you are. Hammering vallys in work. Disgrace of a boy!

Dio ddim yr amser I prygethu! - This not the time to preach.

Gwell bo' nhw'm yn deutha dad fi de cont! - They better not tell my dad cont!

Tyd flaen a neutha nhw ddim - Hurry up and they won't!

Printed in Great Britain
by Amazon

34413640R00119